W9-BET-496

Ben stared at her.

"You don't seriously imagine the fact that you've cast off your fiancée recommends you to me? On top of," Olivia added precisely and with a lot more feeling, "the shameful scam you pulled about how much of your memory was actually lost."

There was a long silence. Then Ben said coolly, "Would you rather I propositioned you differently?"

She frowned at him.

"I could offer to buy a share of Wattle Creek rather than the whole caboodle, on one condition. That you consented to be my mistress."

Amnesia

**What the memory has lost,
the body never forgets**

An electric chemistry with
a disturbingly familiar stranger....
A reawakening of passions long forgotten....
And a compulsive desire to get to know this
stranger all over again!

A brand-new miniseries from
Harlequin Presents® featuring top-selling authors:
Lindsay Armstrong, Penny Jordan
and **Susan Napier**

In September, don't miss
Back in the Marriage Bed
by
Penny Jordan
Harlequin Presents®
#2129

Lindsay Armstrong

OUTBACK MISTRESS

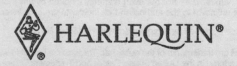

TORONTO • NEW YORK • LONDON
AMSTERDAM • PARIS • SYDNEY • HAMBURG
STOCKHOLM • ATHENS • TOKYO • MILAN • MADRID
PRAGUE • WARSAW • BUDAPEST • AUCKLAND

If you purchased this book without a cover you should be aware that this book is stolen property. It was reported as "unsold and destroyed" to the publisher, and neither the author nor the publisher has received any payment for this "stripped book."

ISBN 0-373-12124-5

OUTBACK MISTRESS

First North American Publication 2000.

Copyright © 2000 by Lindsay Armstrong.

All rights reserved. Except for use in any review, the reproduction or utilization of this work in whole or in part in any form by any electronic, mechanical or other means, now known or hereafter invented, including xerography, photocopying and recording, or in any information storage or retrieval system, is forbidden without the written permission of the publisher, Harlequin Enterprises Limited, 225 Duncan Mill Road, Don Mills, Ontario, Canada M3B 3K9.

All characters in this book have no existence outside the imagination of the author and have no relation whatsoever to anyone bearing the same name or names. They are not even distantly inspired by any individual known or unknown to the author, and all incidents are pure invention.

This edition published by arrangement with Harlequin Books S.A.

® and TM are trademarks of the publisher. Trademarks indicated with ® are registered in the United States Patent and Trademark Office, the Canadian Trade Marks Office and in other countries.

Visit us at www.eHarlequin.com

Printed in U.S.A.

CHAPTER ONE

OLIVIA LOCKHART pushed the damp tendrils of fair hair off her face and flapped the front of her red and cream checked blouse. She was sitting on a fence in the feed shed, an open-sided structure with a corrugated-iron roof, and there were four children gathered around her. 'So,' she said, 'we need to be extra careful—'

She paused as two more children ran up panting—twins, a boy and a girl with identical gingery curls, freckles and gap-toothed smiles as well as a reputation for being able to get into more trouble than Flash Gordon, as the saying went on the station. 'What have you two been up to?' she asked resignedly.

'Nothing! Nothing *bad*,' Ryan Whyte replied with an injured air and turned to his sister Sonia for confirmation.

She nodded her head energetically. 'But, Livvie—'

'Not now, Sonia; let me finish first—we can't afford to waste water—'

'But, Livvie—'

'Sonia, just do as you're told for once—where have you been anyway?'

'Down in the horse paddock, and—'

'Well, you shouldn't be down there on your own. Your father would be very cross. Where was I?' She paused and scanned the faces of the youngsters she was giving this lecture on water conservation to, all children of families who lived and worked on the cattle station. 'That's right—until it rains again we *really* have to—'

'But, Livvie, we found a man,' Sonia said stubbornly.

'We really have to be very careful we don't waste water and—'

'He's dead!' Ryan said.

It took a moment for this to sink in then Olivia jumped off the fence and said warningly, 'If you two are making this up—'

'No, Livvie, he's lying on the ground and he's bleeding. He won't move. We poked him with a stick but nothing happened.'

'He's not dead,' Olivia said thankfully as she knelt in the dusty paddock beneath a burning blue sky. 'But he is unconscious and he's got a nasty gash on his temple.' She reached for a dressing from the first-aid kit they'd brought. 'Who on earth is he and how did he get here?'

Jack Bentley, who was the station foreman, removed his broad-brimmed hat and scratched his head. 'Never seen him in my life before. But we'd better get him up to the homestead and get some attention for him. It's not even as if there's a stray horse around.' He put his hand above his eyes and scanned the paddock.

'Curiouser and curiouser,' Olivia murmured. 'Here, I'll take his feet.'

But it was quite an effort. The stranger was at least

six feet tall and well-built and although they were as careful as could be it was not that easy to ease him onto the back of the Land Rover. He remained deeply unconscious, however.

Olivia climbed into the back with him while Jack drove them to the house and she studied the man narrowly at the same time. She thought he would be in his early thirties and she got the feeling his eyes would be blue—he had thick black hair but a fair, though sunburnt complexion. His face, grimy, blood-stained and cut though it was, was good-looking in a lean way, smooth now but giving a hint of being arresting…

The rest of him, clad in a torn khaki boiler suit, was equally impressive—long and strong-looking but with not an ounce of extra flesh.

Olivia frowned then began cautiously to feel through his pockets but apart from some money and a handkerchief they yielded nothing. She shook her head and murmured, 'Whoever you are, I hope you don't have amnesia because it's almost as if you dropped in from another planet!'

Two hours later, the flying doctor straightened and regarded the strange man with a frown. They'd put him in a guest bedroom and between them, Jack and the doctor, they'd removed his boiler suit and, with Olivia's help, washed him. Then the doctor had stitched his temple but nothing they'd done had caused him to stir.

'Is he in a coma?' Olivia asked worriedly as she

regarded the recumbent figure on the wide bed beneath a clean white sheet.

'Looks like it. He's also got a bump on the head as big as the Opera House but all his vital signs are OK. Uh—I'd say he's a bit dehydrated so I'm going to have to set up a drip— Hang on!'

They all moved closer as the man stirred, muttered something and his eyelids fluttered open.

They *were* blue, Olivia noted—a deep blue but also completely blank. 'Where—the hell am I?' he said with an effort.

It was the doctor who explained, adding ruefully, 'The thing is, we don't know how you came to be here.'

'What…what state?'

'Queensland—Central Queensland. Does that ring a bell?'

But those blue eyes blinked dazedly then the man said, 'Would you believe, I can't seem to remember my name…?' And he struggled suddenly to sit up at the same time as Olivia felt a start of guilt, almost as if she'd wished amnesia on this man.

They had an urgent conference on the veranda.

'Only temporary amnesia, I'd hazard,' the doctor said. 'He has had an almighty bump on the head. If that's the case it will come back to him gradually and we have no real problems. We'll have to keep the fluids up to him and keep him quiet; he's bound to have concussion—think you can cope, Livvie?'

'Of course but—' Olivia gestured a little helplessly

'—what if it isn't temporary? Shouldn't we airlift him to a hospital?'

'I honestly don't think it's necessary at this stage and, to complicate matters, we're really stretched at the moment. I was on my way to pick up someone with a badly broken leg when I intercepted your call and the other aircraft has gone to check out a suspected outbreak of meningitis. But if nothing comes back in a day or two that's what we will do. If you're worried, don't hesitate to call, though. Somehow or other we'll work something out—is your uncle home?'

'No, he's in Japan with a beef marketing delegation but—' she shook her head '—Jack can help me if I need it. We'll have to alert the police, though.' She paused and frowned. 'He must have ridden over from a neighbouring property and his horse—perhaps it threw him and bolted home?'

'Sounds reasonable,' Jack agreed. 'I'll get on to it.'

'Are you a nurse?'

Olivia straightened and looked down at her patient. 'No. But I've had extensive first-aid training—how do you feel?' She smoothed the sheet and sat down beside the bed.

'Terrible,' he said with a wry smile twitching his lips. 'A king-size headache, hot all over, aching like the devil and my tongue seems to be twice its normal size.'

'That's because you're dehydrated and sunburnt—you really shouldn't wander around this countryside without a hat—and the headache comes from a spectacular bump on your head and three stitches in your temple. Otherwise you're fine, apparently.'

He grimaced and winced. 'What about this *fog* I'm living in?'

'Temporary amnesia,' Olivia said promptly and with more assurance than she actually felt. 'The doctor reckons it'll all come back to you gradually.'

'I hope to hell he's right.' He moved restlessly and Olivia got up to plump up his pillows so he could be more comfortable. It was late afternoon and rays from the setting sun were creeping in through the veranda doors and giving a gilded outline to the bed and the lovely old pieces of furniture in the high-ceilinged room. The clock-clocking of a couple of guinea fowl could be heard as they rustled amongst flowering shrubs below the wooden veranda. And Olivia herself was gilded by the rays of the sun.

He studied her, taking in the fair, flyaway hair escaping from the knot at the back of her head and worn with a fringe, the clear-cut sweep of her jaw and slender neck, her grey eyes and creamy skin, her capable hands and outfit of red and cream checked shirt and long khaki trousers. And something crossed those blue eyes although she couldn't read it.

He said, 'Could you tell me a bit more about yourself and this place?'

'If you drink all of this first.' She picked up a glass from the bedside table and offered it to him.

He wrinkled his brow. 'It tastes awful!'

'It's an electrolyte solution to replace all the minerals and salts you lost—look at it this way, you could be hooked up to a drip instead.'

'And you *should* have been a nurse,' he countered with a wicked little glint in his eye.

'Take it or leave it!' she said, but with a grin.

He drank the lot and pulled a face.

Olivia sat down again. 'Well, I'm Olivia Lockhart and you're on Wattle Creek Station. My uncle owns it—he's overseas at the moment—but I've lived here all my life and I help to run it—'

'How old are you?'

'Twenty-five—and we breed—'

He broke in again, with a frown this time. 'Haven't you done anything else? I must say you don't look like the essential jillaroo.'

'Nevertheless I am.' She paused and eyed him.

'What?' he asked gravely but with his eyes laughing at her.

'I just wondered whether you were going to keep interrupting me, Mr...well...whatever your name is.'

'We might have to invent one for the time being. I don't really relish being cast as the man with no name,' he said whimsically.

Olivia considered. 'How would it be if I called you...well, you could have a choice—Tom, Dick or Harry?'

He looked hurt. 'Surely you can do better than that—that would *really* make me feel like a stray mongrel!'

She laughed then sobered. 'Have you *no*...? No, strike that, I—'

'No idea? I really don't,' he said pensively, 'and it's a bloody awful feeling if you must know.'

'Don't strain yourself,' Olivia said contritely. 'I'm

sure it's better to let it come naturally and you're right, I can do better than Tom, Dick or Harry. I'll start at the top of the alphabet,' she said humorously. 'Let's see. Adam, Adrian, Alexander—you couldn't feel like a stray with that name, uh—Arnold, Alfred—'

'Hang on,' he said abruptly. 'Arnold—you know I do believe my name is Benedict…Ben…Ben…' But nothing else came and he swore and collapsed against the pillows.

'That's terrific,' Olivia enthused. 'It shows your memory is coming back. Ben, short for Benedict! But you just relax now,' she ordered.

'Yes, ma'am,' he murmured wryly. 'If you go on telling me about yourself.'

'There's not a lot more to tell—'

'There must be,' he interrupted. 'How come you're not all dry and crinkled?'

'I…' Olivia paused and discovered she felt self-conscious as that blue gaze roamed her face and figure again then came back to her face. 'I've always taken good care of my skin—' she shrugged '—used sunblock and a hat, long sleeves et cetera. My mother used to do the same. But—' her lips curved '—I'm as tough as any other jillaroo underneath it.'

'And you haven't ever done anything else?' he queried.

'Yes, and I still do.' She folded her hands but didn't elaborate.

'If you don't tell me,' he murmured, 'I'll get all hot and bothered again.'

She looked at him narrowly. 'I've got the feeling

you're a genius at getting your own way, Benedict Arnold—that's something you don't seem to have forgotten.'

But he only gazed at her innocently.

She sighed. 'Heaven knows why it's of any interest—'

'It's not every day I get nursed by someone as attractive as you, Olivia Lockhart.'

She bit her lip then saw that glint of wicked amusement in his eyes again. 'OK. I spent three years at university doing an arts course and I paint and design greeting cards if you must know. I've also all but restored Wattle Creek homestead—' she looked around '—to its former glory. I'm passionate about old homes and old things. That's all there is to it. Satisfied, Ben?' she asked laconically.

'No. But certainly interested—what kind of greeting cards?'

'Ones with outback scenes on them or the local flora and fauna; those kind.'

'I'm impressed,' he said. 'You seem to live a very useful and productive life. Is there a Mr Olivia Lockhart?' His gaze strayed to her bare left hand. 'Ah, I see not, unless you don't wear your ring all the time.'

'There is no Mr Olivia Lockhart,' Olivia said coolly, and stopped as whispers and footsteps made themselves heard on the veranda. She listened for a moment then stood up and regarded her patient a little maliciously. 'But I'm sure you wouldn't mind reassuring those who found you that you're not dead.

I'm told that when they poked you with a stick you didn't respond so they thought you were.'

An inward tremor of laughter shook her as she saw his eyes almost cross at this revelation. Then she said, 'Come in, Ryan and Sonia! This is Ben.'

The twins tiptoed in and came to the bedside.

'Glory be,' the man called Ben said, 'what have we here? A case of double trouble if ever I saw one.'

'You're not wrong,' Olivia murmured.

'They're not yours, are they?'

'No. Their parents work on the property.'

'He can talk,' Ryan said to Sonia. 'You couldn't talk when we found you,' he said reproachfully to Ben.

'We thought you were dead!' Sonia added. 'You frightened six months out of us.'

'I do apologize. I must have knocked myself out somehow or other. But I'm very grateful you found me, extremely grateful.'

The twins looked gratified and Ryan said, 'That means we won't get a belting for being in the horse paddock. Doesn't it, Livvie?' He turned to Olivia for reassurance.

'Ryan, you know very well you don't get belted. Your dad just worries about your safety. There could be snakes, anything out there.'

'He can make it feel like a belting even if he doesn't do it, Livvie,' Sonia said earnestly. 'He can make you feel this high.' She demonstrated a distance of about an inch between her thumb and forefinger.

'And that's why you take so much notice of him,' Olivia said sternly although she was trying not to laugh. 'But in this instance we'll forget about it. Off you go!'

'Bye, Mr Ben!' they chorused, and scampered out.

'This paddock with the snakes and—anything in it; how do you think I got there?' Ben asked perplexedly.

'The only thing I can think of is that you rode over from a neighbouring property and your horse—' she shrugged '—got a fright and threw you then bolted home.'

'I've never been thrown by a horse in my life— well, not since I was ten!'

'How do you know?' Olivia asked.

'I…just know,' he said frustratedly.

'But it can happen to anyone,' Olivia objected. 'I mean it *could* have been a snake. Anyway Jack, our station foreman, is making enquiries. He's also getting in touch with the police— Look, you don't look too well again. Why don't you rest?'

'I don't feel well!' He moved uncomfortably and his face contorted with pain.

'Then I'll give you one of these pills; it'll help— now don't make a fuss,' she recommended smoothly. 'I know men can be dreadful patients but it doesn't become you.'

Dark blue eyes stared into hers, angry dark blue eyes, and their owner said, 'Bloody hell—how old do you take me for, Olivia Lockhart?'

'Thirty-something? All the more reason to behave yourself.' She handed him the pill and poured some water into the glass from a jug and handed him that, and simply watched him calmly.

He hesitated then swallowed the pill with the help of the water.

'Good.' She took the glass back and indicated a little silver bell on the bedside table. 'I'm going to start dinner but if you need anything just ring that. Don't you dare get out of bed; is that understood?'

'I was wrong,' Ben said bitterly. 'You should have been a major-general.'

She smiled faintly and placed a cool hand on his forehead. 'Go to sleep, I'm sure things will look better when you wake up.'

He slept through dinner and beyond.

Jack Bentley came up as she was eating her meal at the kitchen table and she invited him to have coffee with her. 'Any news?' she asked as she took two cups and saucers down from the old-fashioned dresser.

'Not a skerrick. No one in the district seems to know him or have anyone unaccounted for. The police are making enquiries; I gave them a description—by the way, Livvie, there is one possibility that's of interest. They've had heavy rain in the next shire, a couple of inches in three hours, and there are a few roads cut. It could be that he got bogged, decided to walk somewhere and got bushed, but—'

'Oh, Jack,' she breathed, 'is it headed this way?'

'Sure is!' He nodded enthusiastically. 'There's a low pressure system that might just do the trick but—' he gestured '—you know how capricious they can be! Good rain fifty miles away doesn't mean it'll hit here although it will seep down eventually which is good news.'

'Let's hold thumbs.' Olivia poured some fragrant coffee from the yellow enamel pot that had been bubbling on the Aga. 'I was just lecturing all the kids about wasting water this afternoon.' She stopped and sighed. 'Another drought would be the last thing we need on top of, well, all else.'

'Low beef prices, currency fluctuations, you name it,' he said.

'Still, Wattle Creek has survived for a long time,' Olivia said, and brushed back her fringe.

'Uh-huh,' Jack murmured noncommittally. 'Doesn't get us much further forward with this bloke, though. How is he?'

'Out like a light—but he's OK. I've been checking his pulse regularly. He can remember his name—his first name anyway. It's Benedict.'

'Got the feeling it might be something fancy.'

'Oh. Did you?' Olivia looked a question at him over the rim of her cup.

'He sounded kinda upper class.' Jack shrugged.

She grimaced. 'I suppose so. He's also quite sure no horse would be game to throw him.'

Jack grinned. 'Cocky as well?'

'Rather sure of himself despite his lack of memory—yes, you could say so,' Olivia responded with a certain amount of feeling.

Jack raised an eyebrow. 'Need a hand? I can stay up here tonight.'

'No, but thanks all the same, Jack.' She stopped as the kitchen door swung and the curtains flapped. 'The wind is getting up.' She put her hands to the side of her head. 'Let's pray it's blowing that depression this way.'

Jack got up. 'I'd best get going then and check everything's tied down and covered up. See you in the morning, Livvie. Don't forget to give me a call if Mr Benedict gets to be a handful.'

Olivia did the dishes and tidied the kitchen.

It was a large, old-fashioned kitchen dominated by the huge old dresser with its colourful display of crockery. There was also a big table and a wooden airing rack suspended from the ceiling where she hung pots and baskets and upside-down bunches of flowers, herbs and leaves she was drying.

The walls were pale yellow, the curtains yellow with white daisies, and at the opposite end to the dresser there was a long narrow table against the wall upon which stood her collection of old implements, an old mincer, a wooden box grinder, a set of brass scales, old biscuit and other tins from a bygone era and her collection of blue and white Spode Regency plates. The floor was green-tiled and the ladder-backed chairs at the table had rush seats.

Although Wattle Creek homestead had other, more formal rooms, the kitchen was the nerve centre of the house.

Then she stepped outside and sniffed the air. It was definitely a restless night, and to her infinite satisfaction, clouds obscured the moon. She went back inside and did a tour through the old homestead, closing doors that led onto the verandas.

And she went to check her patient.

She'd left a lamp on in his room but shaded the bed side of it with a small towel. She could see that he was still asleep although it was a restless kind of sleep and she stared down at him thoughtfully. He wore a pair of her uncle's pyjamas but they were too short and too wide for him and were twisted and rucked around him—her uncle had a large girth, which this man did not, but there was nothing she could do about that. So she concentrated on his face with its lean lines, sunburnt skin and dark shadows on his jaw.

And she thought that he looked vulnerable in this uneasy sleep but, given the things he'd said, she had the feeling that vulnerable was not a state that normally applied to him. Yet, for some reason, she found that she was touched by this man, and she put a hand out and laid it gently on his brow.

He muttered unintelligibly then reached up and grasped her wrist and pulled her hand down to his mouth, and kissed her palm. At the same time his blue eyes fluttered open and he said, 'Sweetheart, I...' And stopped abruptly.

Olivia froze and tried to pull away but his fingers tightened on her wrist.

Then he released a breath and said, 'If it isn't Major-General Lockhart.'

'None other,' she replied tartly. 'Sorry to disappoint you.'

'I didn't say that. Can't think of anyone else I'd rather have soothing my fevered brow at the moment.'

'Will you let me go?'

'Have I offended you?' he countered.

'No... I mean, no, of course not.' She reclaimed her hand.

'You looked entirely disapproving, however,' he commented.

'Who knows how far you could have gone under the misapprehension I was a "sweetheart" of some kind?' she murmured dryly, and pulled a chair up. 'How do you feel?'

He studied her enigmatically for a moment and ignored the question. 'Ever been a "sweetheart" of any kind, Olivia?'

'That's none of your business,' she said evenly. 'Let's just concentrate on how you are.'

He raised an eyebrow. 'Do I detect a reservation on the subject of your love life? As if it mightn't have been that pleasurable an experience?'

Olivia breathed exasperatedly. 'Look, you may as well be the man in the moon for all I know—you don't, surely, expect me to tell you my life story!'

'I may as well be the man in the moon for all *I* know,' he said with a sudden frown. But added with a wry twist of his lips, 'It would help to pass the time.'

'Then you're destined to be disappointed—I have no intention of passing the time that way with you. Will you tell me how you *are* or will I get Jack Bentley up to take over from me?'

'The man who wasn't the doctor?'

'None other,' she said sweetly. 'He's our station foreman and I can assure you he has a heart of gold but—' she gestured '—well, he's very good at roping and throwing calves, I'm just not sure how gentle he is with patients.'

'You wouldn't do that to me, would you, Olivia?' He looked at her reproachfully.

'I most certainly would. So just get your mind off my love life, Mr Benedict Arnold, and tell me how you are!'

He laughed softly. 'Yes, ma'am. Apologies, ma'am! You know, I don't know about Benedict Arnold; he was a traitor if you care to recall.'

'It's not my fault your first name is Benedict,' she retorted, and went to stand up.

'Uh—how am I?' he said hastily. 'Slightly better in some areas than when I reported to you last. My headache has eased a bit and I even appear to be a bit hungry.'

She sank back. 'That's good. I kept some dinner for you. Thirsty?'

'Uh—yes,' he said cautiously. 'However, that presents another problem.'

'I don't think so, you should be thirsty—'

'On the other hand, the copious amounts of liquid you've forced down me have made me highly uncomfortable in another area, I regret to say. May I get up?'

'Oh, that,' Olivia said matter-of-factly. 'No, you may not. I'll—'

'Olivia, I have to tell you that I may be the man from the moon but I do have some modesty—you could be the woman from the moon for all I know.'

'I have no intention of making you blush,' Olivia said with a wicked little glint of her own. 'But the doctor warned me not to let you get up too soon because if you black out I will have the devil's own job to get you back to bed—apart from any further injury you may do to yourself.'

'I see.' The man called Ben eyed her with suspicion. 'So what do you suggest?'

'That I bring you a receptacle, then retire discreetly,' she answered serenely.

'How very practical,' he murmured.

'I told you—well, I didn't go into details, but I did do an extensive first-aid course while I was at university because it's so handy when you live beyond the black stump. I even had hospital experience as a nursing aide.'

'I see,' he said again.

'What now?' she enquired as his eyes lingered on her thoughtfully.

'Nothing. Other than a reinforcement of my earlier sentiment on how useful and productive a person you are. So, I don't have to worry about outraging *your* maidenly modesty?'

'No.'

'That *was* another reason for my reticence—'

'Can I tell you something?' Olivia interrupted, and proceeded to do so. 'You talk too much. Heaven alone knows what you're like when you're fully fit!' And she walked out.

Half an hour later, she brought him a light meal.

He struggled to sit up and she put some more pillows behind him. 'I'm as weak as a kitten,' he said with considerable irritation.

'Some food will help. There's soup and a ragout of chicken.' She lifted the covers off the two dishes.

'Mmm.' He inhaled with evident pleasure. 'I guess cooking is another of your skills.'

'A lot of people cook,' she responded, and handed him a napkin.

'Tell me a bit more about Wattle—Creek, is it?'

Olivia hesitated then sat down beside the bed. 'Yes, well, it's been in the Lockhart family for a hundred years. My uncle runs it now; my father was his brother but he and my mother were killed in a car accident when I was twelve.'

'Do you have a share in it?'

Olivia hesitated again then thought that this had to be better than discussing her love life with a perfect stranger. 'Yes, but my father was a younger brother so my uncle has the controlling share.'

'Central Queensland,' Ben said musingly. 'I've got the feeling I know a lot about it but I can't think why. So...' he paused and turned his attention to the chicken '...in a hundred years I imagine Wattle Creek has had its fair share of drought, flood, pestilence, fire—as well as the good times?'

'It's survived,' Olivia said with simple pride, 'and will go on surviving.'

He lifted his blue gaze to her and frowned. 'Sometimes it can be a whole new ball game; things change,' he said slowly.

'I'm sure they can,' she conceded, 'but we Lockharts are a tough bunch.'

'Tell me a bit more about your uncle. Does he have an heir?'

'Yes, me at the moment,' she said, and grinned. 'He never married. He's a crusty old curmudgeon when he wants to be but I love him dearly.'

'There won't be a Lockhart to carry on the family name?'

She shrugged. 'Not unless I can persuade any future husband of mine to change his name, no. But there'll still be Lockhart blood in our children.'

'Would you do that?' he asked curiously.

'What?'

'Get a future husband to change his name?'

She regarded him gravely. 'Why not?'

'It seems an extreme length to go to—family pride can be, well, too much of it can be dangerous.'

'You say that because you're a man.'

He looked at her quizzically. 'And you could get a reputation for wearing the pants.'

'I probably have that reputation already,' she said prosaically.

He raised an eyebrow. 'You don't mind?'

She smiled coolly at him but reflected inwardly that, while it had never crossed her mind to ask a future husband to change his name until this man had suspected it of her, the lack of a man in her life could just have something to do with an unfeminine, no doubt, unwillingness to have to rely on any man.

'What does that mean?' he queried.

'I—' she shrugged '—like being independent.'

'I believe you.'

Her lips twitched. 'I wouldn't be surprised if you're extremely independent.'

He looked comically surprised. 'What makes you say that?'

'I don't know.' She wrinkled her brow. 'Just a feeling I get, that's all. Perhaps it's because you're so sure no horse would be game enough to throw you.'

He pushed his plate away and lay back against the pillows. 'I've got the feeling you could be right.'

'As well as being a right handful,' Olivia commented.

'I'm sure I don't know what gave you that impression!'

She laughed. 'You don't fool me for a moment, Ben.'

'I wasn't aware that I was trying to but I shall remember that for future reference,' he said ruefully.

'Like a cup of coffee—or perhaps you ought to have tea? Coffee might keep you awake.'

'No, thanks; I don't drink either.'

Olivia raised an eyebrow.

'Don't ask me how I know,' he said frustratedly, 'I just do.'

'I wasn't—going to ask you that. It just seems strange. Do you remember what you do drink?'

'Well, I don't think I'm a teetotaller; a nice cold beer wouldn't go astray—'

'No chance,' she said.

'You are? A teetotaller? Is this a dry establishment?' he asked with some foreboding.

'Not at all. But beer is a diuretic and since we're trying to achieve the opposite it's out of the question. How about a long cold glass of milk?'

'Now that,' he said slowly, 'sounds lovely.'

Olivia regarded him with a mixture of amusement and wryness. 'You're a bundle of surprises, Ben!' She got up, took the tray and went to get him a glass of milk.

'What now?' he asked when he'd finished it.

'Sleep,' she said promptly. 'I don't know about you but I've been up since the crack of dawn—' She stopped and raised her head. 'Was that thunder?'

'It sounded like it.'

'Glory be—and rain!' She walked to the veranda door and peered outside. Big droplets were pattering on the tin roof.

'You need rain?'

She turned back to him. 'Desperately if we're to have a good season. Our dams and creeks are drying up, the feed in the paddocks is withering—oh, do we need rain.'

He looked at her narrowly and seemed about to say something then appeared to change his mind. At least his manner changed and he said lightly, 'Perhaps I've brought you good luck, Olivia.'

She grimaced. 'Perhaps you have, Ben. OK—is there anything else I can do for you? If you're not feeling sleepy would you like to read for a while or—'

'No, thanks.' He yawned suddenly and lay back against the pillows. 'Heaven knows why but I feel extremely sleepy.'

'Good. Now, I'm just next door and I'll leave my door open so don't hesitate to call or ring your bell if you have any problems. Goodnight.'

'Goodnight, Florence Nightingale,' he murmured, but when she looked fleetingly annoyed he said,

'Don't be cross, Olivia. I think you're magnificent and I'm extremely grateful to you.'

She hesitated then walked out with a faint shrug.

She had a shower and sat at her dressing table to brush her hair in a thoughtful, slightly keyed-up mood although she wasn't sure why she should be keyed up. Unless, she mused, it's the wonderful sound of good, heavy rain on the roof?

She put her silver-backed brush down and looked around her bedroom. It had been her parents' bedroom so the bed was double and had lovely curved, cherry-wood ends. The walls were papered in blue and white, a delicate tracery of blue tendrils and flowers on a white background, and the bedspread and curtains matched. She'd found and restored a cherry-wood dressing table with a cheval-mirror and there was a marvellous tallboy chest of drawers.

The carpet was sapphire-blue and there were framed miniatures on the walls that she'd painted herself, framed photos, some of them sepia with age, and a collection of silver and glass perfume bottles on the tallboy. Two big pillows covered in Battenberg lace sat at the head of the bed.

But her bedroom didn't afford her the usual satisfaction and she turned back to the mirror with a sigh. Be honest, Livvie, she told herself. It was the look in his eye when he told you you were magnificent that's caused you to feel keyed up.

She grimaced at her reflection but it didn't alter the distinct impression she'd got that he hadn't been alluding to her nursing skills when he'd said it.

Somehow or other he'd managed to combine a tribute to her face and figure in that lazy blue glance.

She looked down at her hands then forced herself to study herself in the mirror.

True, her skin was good, the colour of her hair was like ripe wheat, her grey eyes were clear, her lashes long and dark-tipped, her neck long and her figure lithe and trim. True, when she took the trouble, she could look elegant and—someone had once told her— refined. But she'd never considered herself especially attractive. And she rarely bothered to dress up... Always too busy doing something else, she reflected with a spark of amusement.

But she sobered almost immediately. And nearly always too busy to worry much about men, she added to herself. So *why* should a perfect stranger suddenly produce this reaction?

Anyway, how dare he, when all he can remember is his first name, be sending me those kind of looks?

She got up and smoothed her navy pyjamas piped with white, and got into bed. Think about the rain, she commanded herself. Don't let it stop too soon— if the power of thought can do it!

CHAPTER TWO

A COUPLE of hours later she was woken by a crash.

She flew out of bed and saw light flood into the passage from the guest bedroom. 'Don't tell me you've fallen out of bed,' she muttered, and raced into the next room.

But Ben was sitting up dazedly in bed with his hand still on the lamp switch—and the cause of the crash became obvious. One of the veranda doors was swinging dementedly as rain blew into the room.

'Damn! I mustn't have closed it properly when I looked out earlier.' She ran across the room and with an effort pushed the door closed against the wind and latched it. 'Sorry.' She turned to the bed and shook raindrops off herself. 'That's probably the last thing you needed—things that go bang in the night.'

'I...' he lay back '...couldn't work out where the hell I was. That's quite a storm.'

'Yes. I just hope it's not all talk—you all right? You look pale.' She stood beside the bed and frowned down at him.

'I'm OK—well, relatively.'

'How about—how about a nip of brandy? I think I could do with one myself. I thought the roof was falling in.'

'What a fine suggestion, Olivia.'

So she got two nips in crystal tumblers and sat down beside the bed.

'Storms don't bother you?' he queried.

'No.' She took a sip of brandy. 'I like them.'

'Silly question,' he murmured.

'Do they bother you?' Olivia asked.

'Contrary to all manly norms, they do a bit. I once saw a bolt of lightning strike a horse and I've never been the same since. Although I don't have to scuttle under beds these days.'

Olivia laughed. 'I don't believe you.'

'You should.'

'Where was this horse?'

He screwed up his face. 'I can't remember but—'

'Don't try,' she said immediately. 'Sorry I asked. Have some brandy instead.'

He looked at her ruefully then his eyes changed. 'There is one thing better than scuttling under a bed in a storm.'

'What's that?'

'Having someone *in* bed with you who you can cuddle up to.'

Olivia blinked, and in the pause that developed as his gaze roamed over her navy pyjamas and her loose hair she was astounded to have a clear image in her mind of—just that. She swallowed and coughed. 'You—you're an incredibly quick worker, Benedict Arnold!'

'Seize the moment—someone said. I think it would be rather nice. Might just get me off to sleep again, which isn't going to happen otherwise,' he added pointedly.

'Oh, yes, it is. I'll give you another of those pills.'

'Dear Olivia, don't do that to me,' he said plaintively. 'I hate being drugged. You have no idea how lousy you feel when you wake out of it.'

'Well, I'm certainly not getting into bed with you—you must be mad,' she said helplessly.

He smiled slightly and although his scratches were visible, his lips dry and cracked, and despite the dark shadows on his jaw, it was, Olivia found herself thinking, one of the most arresting, vital faces she'd ever seen.

He said, 'Considering that I am wounded, that I've lost my memory and hate storms—' he winced at a crack of thunder '—could you stay and talk to me for just a bit? You do look thoroughly wide awake yourself.'

'I—' She bit her lip and contemplated that she was thoroughly wide awake, as well as thinking how awful it might be to be lying awake in the dark wondering who you were. 'All right. Just for a bit, though. I'll go and get a dressing gown.'

'To curb any further improper suggestions I might make?' he queried gravely.

'Because I'm cold, but that too,' she retorted, and marched out.

She came back wearing a white terry towelling robe and with socks on and a tartan rug over her arm. She pulled a more comfortable armchair up to the bed, and a footstool, stretched herself out and put the rug over her. Then she picked up her brandy and said, 'Sure you're warm enough?'

'Quite, thank you,' he said politely.

'What shall we talk about?'

'Well, there's nothing I can tell you about me so it will have to be you.'

'I've told you all I intend to tell you about me.' Olivia shot him a cutting little grey glance.

'Not even in general terms?' he said. 'Your ambitions, your plans—unless they *are* all bound up with Wattle Creek?'

She sighed and laid her head back. 'You don't have to make it sound so…limited.'

'Did I? My apologies. How old did you say you were, Olivia?'

'Twenty-five. What's that got to do with anything?'

'Nothing *per se* but isn't it about time you thought of providing those heirs for Wattle Creek?'

'You don't need to concern yourself along those lines, Ben.' She studied the amber liquid in the crystal glass then raised her grey eyes to his. 'In fact I find it insufferably prying of you.'

He shrugged but wasn't noticeably dashed. 'Have you ever thought, has it ever occurred to you that men might see you quite differently from how you see yourself?'

Olivia frowned. 'I don't know what you mean.'

'Well, a lot of women don't realize just what men see in them.'

'If I knew what this was leading to I might be able to agree or disagree,' she said humorously. 'But if you're expecting me to ask you how you see me it doesn't bother me one way or the other.'

'No,' he mused. 'Far too independent for that but

I'll tell you anyway. I see a girl a man could take seriously—provided he could ever get to first base. And...' he paused and looked at her with his lips twitching '...for heirs to ensue one needs to do that at least.'

'How do you know no one has done just that?'

'Have they?' He looked at her alertly.

Olivia finished her brandy. 'That's personal not general, Ben.'

'You brought it up!'

'Only because you led me into it— Look,' she said goadedly, 'I'll tell you what I feel then perhaps we can get some relief from this subject! Love is *fine*. I've fallen in love a couple of times and it was—all the things it should be. Except that it didn't last and that was without the pressures of marriage, children and so on. Or the pressure of a bossy boots like me,' she added blithely.

He grinned. But a moment later he said soberly, 'If you ever lost Wattle Creek, though—and these things can happen—what would you do with your life?'

'I'd fight tooth and nail *not* to lose Wattle Creek,' she responded tartly. 'They'd have to drag me off kicking and screaming!' She grimaced. 'But if they did manage to achieve it I've always got my painting and—who knows? I could take up nursing impossibly curious amnesia victims.'

'Thank you,' he murmured.

She gazed at him, opened her mouth then closed it.

'Do tell me, Olivia.' He looked amused.

'I shouldn't really but I couldn't help wondering

whether, amongst the things you *do* remember, there is an attitude towards love and marriage?'

He drained his glass, set it on the table and slipped down the pillows. 'I think it's a fine institution in general. Like you, though, I tend to wonder how the spark stays in it under all the pressures you mentioned, but that could be because neither of us has really fallen in love yet.'

'So you don't think you could be married?'

'I have…no recollection of a wife.' He paused and frowned.

'I keep doing it,' Olivia said contritely. 'Look, I'm sure by tomorrow – well, today—the police will come up with who you are.'

'Let's hope so. In general terms, though, what kind of a wife do you think you'd make?'

'I have no idea—what kind of a husband do you think you'd make?'

'I think I'd be rather good at it,' he said pensively. 'I'm house-trained, I like children and I like women—'

'Not more than one at a time, I hope. That wouldn't make you a good husband.'

'Well, all this is on the basis of having found the *right* one, naturally, but when I say I like women I mean that their little foibles don't irritate me unduly.'

'Such as?' Olivia asked ominously but the glint of laughter in her grey eyes gave her away.

'Their preoccupation with clothes for example. Women are much nicer when they've got the right things to wear and their hair is to their satisfaction et

cetera for all that they may not understand the basics
are what men still see.'

'Do you know, Benedict Arnold, that's a very superior attitude?'

He grinned. 'It's also a wise one, Olivia Lockhart.
So, all in all, *I* think I'd make a nice husband.'

'Your faith in yourself is monumental. *I* think
you'd make a real handful of a husband, Ben.'

'I don't know why you persist with this ''handful''
tag,' he murmured.

'Call it feminine intuition,' she said wryly. 'Not all
of us are so taken up with clothes et cetera that we
can't see past the end of our noses.'

He looked thoughtful. 'Is there anything about men
that drives you mad?'

'I—' she paused '—get on very well with men as
it happens.'

'That could be because you're not one of those ul-
tra-feminine women.'

For a moment her expression defied description
then she started to laugh. 'Many would take exception
to that remark, Ben.'

'Let me explain—'

'I think it would be a good idea—you are a bit
dependent on my goodwill at the moment, you know.'

'Well, there are women you can only think of in
terms of having sex with. I mean to say you really
can't find a lot to talk to them about—'

'What you *really* shouldn't do is go to bed with
women you can't talk to, Ben. There are some very
unkind labels for that kind of man.'

'Unfortunately it's one of the hazards of being a

man, Olivia,' he countered wickedly. 'A predisposition to think along those lines. However, what I was trying to say is that you very obviously have a mind of your own that would be interesting to explore and you don't give off vibes of being sultry and seductive, which is quite a relief, and all in all, as I said earlier, you're a woman a man could take seriously in a variety of ways. Which is to say in bed and out of it.'

She regarded him fixedly for a time. Then she blinked and said, 'You've only known me for a matter of hours!'

'If there's one good thing to be said for having a blank mind it's that it's very receptive to new impressions.'

'And you don't have any qualms about making these kind of declarations to a complete stranger? Don't answer; that was a rhetorical question.'

He grinned. 'Oh, well, Olivia, I've got the feeling I'm not one for beating about the bush.'

'So have I,' she said dryly. 'But here's something for you to think about—any more of this kind of talk and I'll go to bed.'

'Right. Tell me what kind of cattle you breed, how many head you run, what the acreage of Wattle Creek is, capacity, et cetera.'

She opened her mouth but his expression was grave and polite. Her lips twisted, then curved into a reluctant smile. 'Don't think you fool me for a moment but—you asked for it.'

'I'm really interested,' he protested.

Olivia drained the last of her brandy, laid her head back, and started to tell him.

He asked some surprisingly intelligent questions along the way until Olivia was moved to say, 'I think you may know something about this business, Ben.'

'I think I may,' he responded. 'Why and wherefore is another matter.' He stopped and yawned.

'Good time to go to sleep,' she suggested.

'Are you going to abandon me?'

She studied him then said, 'There is something you may not know about me.'

He lifted a sleepy eyebrow.

'I sing,' she said. 'How would it be if I sang you to sleep?'

A look of wariness descended across his expression that made her want to laugh. 'I'll do it very quietly,' she assured him, and started off. '"Git along, little dogie…"'

Her voice was clear and soft and as she sang that old cowboy song she saw him look surprised then relax and within minutes he was asleep.

She contemplated getting up, switching off the lamp and going to bed but discovered she was quite comfortable and feeling sleepy herself. I'll do it in a few minutes, when he's properly asleep, she thought—and that's the last thing she remembered.

It was Jack Bentley who woke them the next morning.

'Livvie—oh, there you are!'

Olivia struggled up in the armchair and Ben opened his eyes.

'What's the problem, Livvie?' Jack asked anxiously, coming into the room and looking at her bewilderedly. 'Has he had—is there...are you OK, mate?' He turned to Ben.

Olivia stood up and stretched. 'He's fine, Jack. Well, he was last night, just couldn't sleep so I kept him company for a while. Any news? Glory be, it's still raining!'

'Not only that but it's flooding,' Jack said. 'We're going to have to move a bit of stock about.'

'Any other news?' Ben said, sitting up with a contorted expression as if he had any number of aches and pains.

'Well, mate, if it means anything to you, there's a flap on about a bloke who went missing in his light aircraft—think it could be you?'

Olivia gasped.

Whereas Ben said slowly, 'Bloody hell. So that's what happened. Yes, I remember now. I had to make an emergency landing in the middle of nowhere; the fuel pump seemed to have gone on the blink. But...but...'

'So the name Bradshaw doesn't mean anything to you?' Jack asked acutely.

'Bradshaw. Bradshaw,' Ben said slowly, and that frown Olivia was coming to know well creased his brow.

'Never mind, it'll come,' she said comfortingly, and turned to Jack with more urgency. 'Just let me get dressed and I'll— Jack, would you mind helping Ben with whatever he needs at the moment? I'll call the police and let them know he's safe and sound. Then we can have a conference.' She gathered up the rug and padded out of the room.

Jack Bentley and Ben Bradshaw watched her go then looked at each other ruefully.

'That is one very capable lady,' Ben said.

'You're not wrong, mate. And very much esteemed on Wattle Creek,' he added with a suddenly straight glance.

'I…get the picture,' Ben Bradshaw said slowly.

'Yep, wouldn't do to try and take advantage of her.'

The patient raised an eyebrow. 'I don't think there's any danger of that; she seems to have her feet firmly planted on the ground.'

'Maybe. Just thought I'd pass it on,' Jack said urbanely. 'So your memory's coming back? Any idea where you made this emergency landing? Not that there's a lot we can do at the moment.'

Ben lay back. 'Not only did the fuel pump pack up but I had a complete electrical failure, so my GPS lost power, and the radio. I do remember hiking for bloody hours. That's right, I'd flown over the homestead a couple of hours earlier so I set off in the direction I remembered it to be in. South-east, so the plane should be north-west of here roughly.'

'Can you remember why you were flying in these parts?'

'I—' But he broke off as Olivia came in. She was dressed in jodhpurs, an oilskin jacket and had a broad-brimmed hat in her hands.

'Ben, you took off from Longreach yesterday morning and you filed a flight plan to return to Longreach in the afternoon. The authorities are getting in touch with your next of kin or whatever but it looks as if you might be stuck with us for a day or two. There's extensive flooding, roads are impassable and telephone lines are cut everywhere and people are stranded, our airstrip is under water and our only form of communication at the moment is the satellite phone.'

'I see. I—'

But Olivia swept on. 'How do you feel?' And she reached for his wrist to check his pulse against her watch.

'A lot better other than a few stiff muscles.'

'No severe headaches, double vision or nausea?' She watched him narrowly as he shook his head, and presented him with a thermometer. 'Open up.'

He did so ruefully.

'No internal pains, no waterworks problems?'

He shook his head again and she pinched the skin of his forearm, appeared satisfied with the result and gently removed the dressing over the stitches on his temple. 'Good,' she said briskly, and applied a fresh one. Then she removed the thermometer and murmured, 'Pretty normal. All the same, stay in bed.'

'Oh, I—'

'Just do as you're told, Benedict Arnold,' Olivia recommended. 'I'm going to have to leave you for a few hours but I'm putting you on your honour. Kay, Jack's wife, is coming up to cook you breakfast and so on—don't give her any trouble. And the flying doctor is going to ring so you can tell him exactly how you feel and how your memory is coming back.'

'Yes, ma'am!' Ben replied, and for some reason cast Jack a bitter little glance.

'What's that supposed to mean?' she enquired.

'Nothing...' They said it together but Jack looked amused.

'Ready, then, Jack?'

'Whenever you are, Livvie.'

They walked out together and Ben Bradshaw watched them go then shook his head somewhat bemusedly. A homely face presently intruded upon his reflections and Kay Bentley came into the room with his breakfast.

It was four-thirty in the afternoon before Olivia returned to the homestead. It was still pouring.

'How is he?' she asked Kay as she came wearily and wetly into the kitchen.

'Good as gold,' Kay said. 'He's been dozing quite a lot but the flying doctor said he could get up later— by the way, Livvie, the satellite phone dropped out.'

Olivia swore beneath her breath.

'I took it down to Davo; he said he'd try and fix it—but he's a lovely man—Ben, I mean,' Kay continued enthusiastically. 'Really grateful with beautiful manners and he made me laugh too.'

'He obviously didn't—' Olivia broke off. Suggest you go to bed with him, she'd been going to say, but thought better of it.

'And I went down and got some of Graham's clothes for him,' Kay continued. Graham was their twenty-year-old son. 'Your uncle's things are miles too wide and short for him,' she added with a chuckle.

'That was kind of you, Kay.' Olivia sat down at the kitchen table. 'You wouldn't believe it but yesterday I was worried about a drought; now I'm worried about too much rain.'

'It's always either a feast or a famine on the land but it can't do any harm in the long run,' Kay offered.

'No, but half-drowned stock in the short term is a problem.'

'I'll make you a cuppa. Eaten anything today?'

Olivia roused herself. 'Not a lot. A bite of breakfast in passing.'

Kay got busy immediately and shortly a cup of tea and plate of cheese and tomato sandwiches were set in front of Olivia.

'Thanks, Kay, you're a brick.'

'I also made you a casserole for dinner. You just need to heat it up. When is your uncle due back?'

'Not for a week. Still, I'm sure we can cope—you wouldn't believe the wretched phone going on the blink!'

'Why don't you relax for a while?' Kay said sympathetically. 'I can hold the fort for an hour or so.'

'I think I'll do just that!'

She didn't actually rest but she had a long hot bath and changed into slim black trousers and a rich tawny shirt with long sleeves. She put her hair up in a knot and thought about trimming her fringe but couldn't be bothered. Then she remembered Ben Bradshaw and as well as smoothing moisturizer into her skin she put on some frosted, bronzey lipstick.

I must be mad, she thought, with a slight smile. What am I trying to do? Prove that I'm not all sober, serious and unseductive?

But he wasn't in the guest bedroom and she found him seated alone at the kitchen table.

'Are you sure—?' she started to say.

'Quite sure,' he broke in, and got up. 'I even have the blessing of the doctor.'

'So Kay said,' she murmured, and studied him. He wore a pair of navy blue jeans and a blue and white checked shirt. His thick, dark hair was brushed and he'd shaved although rather sketchily because of the stitches and scratches on his face. His sunburn was fading.

'You look tired,' he commented.

She grimaced. 'A day in the saddle on top of a broken night can do that to you but I'll be fine.'

'I feel guilty—I not only kept you up but I seem to have brought you too much rain.'

'Time will tell.' She moved past him. 'Country life is a bit like that—either a feast or a famine, as Kay remarked earlier. The problem is there has been rain to the north and although it kept missing us it was flowing into the channels and creeping down towards us. That's why this downpour has caused them to flood.'

'Banjo Paterson country.'

'Yes.' She pulled out a chair. 'But tell me about your day.'

'I didn't accomplish much,' he said ruefully. 'I spoke to the flying doctor then the police but the satellite phone dropped out at that point, I'm sorry to have to tell you, Olivia.'

'So Kay said.' Olivia grimaced. 'It never rains but pours but Davo, our resident mechanic, is a bit of a genius so here's hoping he can fix it. Did you get the chance to find out anything from the police?'

'Well, yes. I am Ben Bradshaw, I work for a pastoralist company, I'm thirty-three, I was on my way to Campbell Downs and I'm based at Charleville.'

Olivia stared at him then got up and took a bottle of wine from the fridge and got two glasses out. 'Congratulations! So there is no fog any more?'

He frowned. 'There are still blank patches but it's starting to get clearer.'

'Thank goodness.' She handed him a corkscrew. 'You do drink wine, don't you?'

'I do.'

'Open that, then, and I'll just pop Kay's casserole in the oven.' She opened the Aga oven with a padded glove and slid the dish in.

'What about family and friends?' she asked as she sat down again and accepted a glass of golden chardonnay from him. 'Cheers, by the way. You're lucky you weren't killed, one way or another.'

'Cheers. And many thanks,' he responded.

'So?'

He raised an eyebrow at her.

'Family and friends,' she reminded him wryly.

'My next of kin, they tell me, is my mother and she's overseas—I remember her—but I guess they'll get in touch with anyone else who might need reassuring—that was when the phone cut out.'

'So you don't have a wife?'

'Apparently not.' But his eyes were amused. 'Why do you ask?'

'She might be horrified to know how your mind works under the influence of temporary amnesia.'

'I didn't think I was that bad.'

It was her turn to look amused. 'You know very well you were.'

'Could be I took one look at you and was slayed, Olivia.'

'I doubt it. I'm twenty-five and I don't usually have that effect on men—as you took pains to explain why to me.'

He sat back and played with the stem of his wine-glass. Then he raised those deep blue eyes to hers. 'I think you look tired but lovely tonight.'

She felt herself colour and found herself speechless for a moment or two. Then she looked away and said, 'Thanks, but I'd rather you said no more.'

'All right. How many head of cattle did you have to move?'

They discussed the situation on the station in detail then the country in general and it took them through Kay's delicious beef and mushroom casserole. Then he asked if she'd show him the homestead.

'With pleasure,' she said warmly.

It was a rambling old house with a huge lounge and dining room separated by a graceful wooden arch. The walls were forest-green, the couches and chairs covered in ruby brocade and the round dining-room table was an early Australian antique. Gold-framed pictures hung on the walls, there was a magnificent grandfather clock and, above the fireplace, the portrait of a fair woman.

'My mother,' Olivia said sadly.

'That must have been dreadful.'

'It was.'

'You look a lot like her.'

'Thanks. But I remember thinking she was truly beautiful. This is my father.' She moved to a smaller portrait in the dining room. 'And this is my uncle Garth.'

'I would—uh—he looks like a tough customer.'

'He is. I could do with him right now.'

'Did you—? No, you couldn't have painted these.'

'No. But, apart from being too young, I'll tell you why when we get to my studio.'

He glanced at her then paused in the doorway to look back at the lovely room. 'You certainly have a knack for decorating.'

She shrugged. 'I had some lovely stuff to work with and you don't find rooms with these proportions so readily these days. This is the morning room, much more modern, and this—' she moved to another doorway '—is my studio. I glassed in a veranda, conservatory style, to give me plenty of light, not that you can appreciate it at the moment.'

In fact rain was beating heavily on the glass but the overhead light was strong and revealed an uncluttered room with a wooden floor, a big table and a couple of stools, a sink and two easels.

'You were going to tell me something,' he said as he wandered over to the easels.

'Ah, yes. For some reason I paint best in miniature. That's why greeting cards suit me so well.'

He turned to her. 'That's...curious.'

'I know. It's inexplicable actually. My mind's eye must have a miniaturizing effect on my brain.'

'But these are good.' He studied a small canvas resting on one easel and a sketch pad on the other. The canvas, in oils, was a scene of ghost gums on a creek bank, while the pad bore a delicate and faithful watercolour reproduction of a pink and grey galah on a branch. 'And this is accurate—are you a naturalist too?'

'In a way. I like to get them right.' She brushed back her fringe. 'I sometimes think that a hundred years ago that's what I might have been, you know, wandering around in a long white dress with a high neck and a cameo brooch, a big hat and a sketch pad.'

'I think that even a hundred years ago you'd have been too energetic for that.'

'Perhaps,' she conceded wryly. 'But ladies were expected to be ladies in those days.'

'I don't think there's much doubt that you're a lady, Olivia.'

She looked at him wryly. 'How can you tell?'

'Well—' he leant against a wall and folded his arms '—you have a certain born-to-command air—'

'You told me yesterday that could be misconstrued as a desire to wear the pants.'

'I've changed my mind about that. You do it— rather regally in fact. Then there's the way you handle impossibly curious, not to mention importuning strangers.'

'I don't know about that either,' Olivia commented ruefully. 'You got me to discuss things with you that

I would normally never dream of discussing with a strange man.'

'That could be because of the electricity between us,' he said idly, but went on before she could take issue. 'All the same, there was still a lot of reserve about you. And you paint, you decorate, you cook like a dream—'

'I didn't cook tonight. That was Kay.'

'But you did last night. Yes.' He straightened. 'I think I'd take you for a lady.'

'I— Some of the best cooks have been men,' she said, irrelevantly, she felt, but she was oddly breathless, she discovered. And unable to tear her gaze from his. But she forced herself to breathe evenly, and to respond more in kind. 'You—I don't know about being a gentleman—but you sound rather upper class, Ben.'

The faintest smile twisted his lips. 'Do I?'

'Yes. Jack was the first to notice it.'

She paused and studied him reflectively. 'But now I come to think of it, you sound very well educated, you speak refinedly and you certainly are quite unabashed by anything, even under the influence of temporary amnesia. That kind of self-possession is often associated with a privileged background. You're born and bred to it, in other words, even if you can't remember it.'

'My mother would be delighted to hear you say so, Olivia, but in fact my father was a blacksmith.'

She blinked.

He looked at her wickedly. 'I'm sorry if I've disappointed you—'

'Of course you haven't. I mean to say—' she heard herself sounding flustered and was sure she looked it '—it means nothing—Oh! Now I feel like a terrible snob which I'm *not*. How did you do this to me?'

He laughed and came to stand right in front of her. 'All *I* was trying to do was compliment you on your class, Olivia.'

'To make up for earlier telling me how unseductive I was,' she remarked dismally.

'That wasn't what I said at all; I'm sorry if I hit a nerve but I *meant* that there was a lot more to you.'

'Heaven alone knows why you should have hit a nerve,' she replied ruefully. 'I don't know you—'

'From a bar of soap,' he finished with a little glint of devilry in his eyes. 'Perhaps this is the reason.'

All he did was touch the back of his hand to her cheek but she was transfixed.

The uproar of the rain on the roof, the familiar setting of her studio, the cares of a cattle station all but under water faded and it was just the two of them standing in a pool of light. But that contact of his hand on her cheek was magnetic and seemed to transmit an awareness of all that was vital, attractive and tantalizing about Ben Bradshaw.

The intensity of it startled her so that her eyes widened because she could never before remember being so physically conscious of a man, so instantly attracted not only to the lean, lithe length of him and his broad shoulders but his wicked sense of humour and the odd little things that she'd learnt about him— that he liked milk, not tea or coffee, that he disliked thunderstorms, his insouciance when all he'd been able to remember was his first name.

Silly things really but for some reason they added up to produce a feeling of tenderness in her as well as the electricity that was sparking between them.

And she couldn't doubt that it was, as his blue gaze roamed down her tawny shirt then lingered on the hollows at the base of her throat. Because it was as if his long fingers were stroking her skin, touching secret, sensitive parts of her body, and it was as if the only relief from the sweet torture of it would be to be in his arms.

I don't believe this, she thought, but her heart was beating heavily under the tawny silk and her breasts started to tingle as his curiously heavy-lidded gaze rested on them. How can I be so aware of him? How can my body respond to a mere touch on my cheek and the way he's looking at me?

'No…' It was the barest whisper but he dropped his hand as she said it, and she moved a step backwards.

'I agree,' he said quietly.

Olivia blinked and swallowed and found her voice. '*What* do we agree about?'

'That we shouldn't rush into anything,' he murmured with some irony.

'Rush…I…you didn't expect…' She closed her mouth.

He raised a wry eyebrow. 'Didn't expect that, although it's what we both want, you would come to bed with me? No. Nor would I ask you. It could just get my face slapped,' he said gravely.

'Don't...don't joke about it,' she warned intensely.

He sobered. 'Then will you tell me what you would like to do, Olivia?'

She stared at him and brushed her fringe aside with her fingers. 'Nothing, Ben. Not until I get to know you better, at least, but I don't even know if that will happen.'

'Why not?'

'Well—' she looked at him a little helplessly '—we don't know whether our lives will run parallel at all.'

He narrowed his eyes. 'Do you mean whether my life will run parallel with Wattle Creek?'

She shrugged defensively. 'I am here and you are in Charleville.'

'That's not what I meant, Olivia, and I think you know it.'

'Ben—' she rubbed her eyes suddenly and shook her head '—I can't...please... This has sprung up out of nothing!'

He stared down at her inscrutably for a long moment then he touched her cheek again but this time it was the briefest touch of his fingers. 'Go to bed. But we *were* in agreement—about not rushing into anything.'

'I...yes. But I just can't go to bed like that. Anyway you should be the one—'

'What did you propose doing?'

'The dishes for one thing, closing up, turning out lights, and I was going to do the ironing—'

'You're not serious?'

'Well...' she hesitated and her shoulders slumped

'...perhaps not the ironing tonight; it could wait but the rest can't.'

'I can do all the rest.'

She opened her mouth then frowned. '*You're* not serious?'

'Perfectly. I told you I was house-trained.'

'I know but...' She trailed off.

'I've also spent most of the day *in* bed and I wouldn't be able to sleep yet. Whereas you are out on your feet. By the way, that's one thing I forgot to add to the list of your ladylike virtues: you sing too. Really well.'

She smiled suddenly. 'If you could have seen your face when I offered to.'

'You did take me by surprise,' he said ruefully.

'I certainly won't need any singing to sleep. Then—' she hesitated again '—if you're sure?'

'Quite sure I can cope with a few dishes and turning the lights out, Olivia.' He watched her with some irony.

She blushed unaccountably but recovered almost immediately. 'Goodnight, Mr Arnold, then,' she said humorously, and offered him her hand.

'Goodnight, Miss Lockhart,' he responded, and they shook hands.

'Don't do too much, though,' she warned. 'I'm sure one should treat a bump that caused even temporary amnesia with care.'

'I'm sure one should and I'll be very careful.'

He let her hand go and they stared at each other for a long moment. Until Olivia turned away.

CHAPTER THREE

SHE fell asleep almost immediately but woke at two in the morning. It was still raining.

The continuing rain didn't occupy her mind as she lay in her parents' bed beneath the blue and white coverlet; Ben Bradshaw did.

What kind of a man is he really? she wondered. I know I attributed his sang-froid to a privileged background but that's not necessarily the way it may be. Anyway, a privileged background is no guarantee of anything. But he is a charming, attractive stranger and the big question is—how indiscriminately does he use that charm? I'd hate to be one of a long line of conquests and his *modus operandi* has to be somewhat suspect—doesn't it?

She moved and frowned in the darkness. It was a long time, she realized, since she'd been attracted to a man. Two or three years, she decided, and thought ruefully that she could be in danger of becoming a dried-up old spinster, let alone a dried-up jillaroo.

Then it occurred to her that she still didn't know what Ben Bradshaw actually did other than work for a pastoral company, or why he should have been on his way to Campbell Downs—a huge, adjoining property, as it happened, that had been sold recently.

I don't know why I didn't think to ask more, she mused, and jumped as a knock sounded on her door.

She sat up, flicked on her lamp and pulled the bed-clothes up to her throat. 'What is it?'

The door opened and Ben stood there. 'Olivia—'

'Oh, look here,' she broke in, 'this is too much! If, for no other reason than simple gratitude, you can't just leave me alone—'

'Olivia—' he advanced into the room '—if you think I've come to seduce you, you're wrong.'

'Well, what am I supposed to think?' she countered.

'I am fully dressed. I am also wet.'

She took all this in. His hair was plastered to his head and Graham's shirt and jeans were not only damp but muddy. 'So?' she said slowly.

'So seduction, I'm sorry to say, was the furthest thing from my mind.' He paused and his dark blue eyes swept over her with some irony.

Olivia released her stranglehold on the bedclothes and lowered them several inches but she tilted her chin at him with hauteur. 'What is the problem, then?'

He looked at her for a long moment with some cynical amusement clearly evident in his eyes. Then he said, 'Your roof is leaking, Miss Lockhart, ma'am. Right over my bed as it happens and, while I'm quite happy to move to another bed, I can't help wondering whether it's a good idea to let it go on leaking.'

Olivia gasped then tossed the bedclothes aside and sprang up. 'Why on earth didn't you say so sooner? Of course it's not a good idea to let it go on leaking, there are electrical wires—'

'You didn't give me the opportunity,' he murmured, and watched as she started to unbutton her pyjama top. Then he said with gentle satire, 'I think I'll leave you to dress on your own.'

'Here,' she said a few minutes later, and handed him a waterproof. She already had hers on and she crammed her felt hat on her head. 'I gather you've been out to investigate?'

'Yes. Not that I could see much. We're going to need a ladder and a tarpaulin.'

'I am. You're not climbing up the roof—'

'I'm perfectly capable of climbing up the roof, Olivia.'

'Your head. Your stitches!' she protested.

'My head is fine and I've taken the liberty of going through your first-aid kit and finding a strong bandage and a waterproof covering for my stitches.' He pointed to his temple.

'Oh. Still, I suppose I could always call Jack but he's had such a big day—he was up hours before he came to get me this morning, they all were so—'

'Lead on, Miss Lockhart,' Ben Bradshaw said firmly.

An hour later a tarpaulin was secured over the patch of the old corrugated-iron roof that was leaking and they were crawling through the roof checking the wiring.

'Seems to be all OK,' Ben said at last, swinging the torch in a wide arc.

'Yes. Yuk,' Olivia replied, and brushed a cobweb away from her face. She shuddered.

'Don't like spiders?'

'As little as you like thunderstorms. Well, I think we've done all we can. Shall we go down?'

'After you, ma'am,' he said courteously.

She climbed down the manhole into the kitchen and heaved a sigh of relief. The Aga was still alight; it served the dual purpose of a water heater as well as a stove and she took off her jacket and hat and warmed herself in front of it. Then she turned to look at Ben and had to laugh. He was wet and black but then, so was she.

'We look like a couple of drowned rats—I don't suppose Kay brought you any other clothes?'

'She did as a matter of fact. A set of pyjamas and another pair of jeans and a shirt.'

'Then I think you should change immediately—have a bath and come back and get warm. The last thing I need is for you to develop pneumonia.'

'I'm actually a lot tougher than I may look,' he murmured. 'How's this for a suggestion? Why don't we both dry off and change then I'll make us some cocoa?'

Olivia looked surprised and opened her mouth to demur but thought better of it. 'All right.'

She had a quick hot shower instead of a bath and came back to the kitchen in her pyjamas and terry towelling robe, drying her hair with a hand towel.

Ben was already there in pyjamas and her uncle's winter dressing gown and the kettle was boiling.

'That was fast work,' she commented.

He turned from the stove. 'I can work fast if necessary.'

'May I have a look at your stitches? It'll be a miracle if you didn't wet them or tear them with all that heaving and lifting you did tonight.

'Hmm,' she said a few minutes later. 'A little red around the edges. I'll put some antiseptic powder on and a new dressing but we'll have to watch them.'

He studied her downcast head as she looked through the first-aid kit, and found himself thinking that he knew of no other woman not only so capable but also so agile and athletic when it came to balancing on wet rooftops, shinning up ladders and crawling through confined spaces.

He said, 'Are you sure you didn't inflict any harm on yourself?'

'Don't think so.' She looked up and blinked at him. 'Well,' she amended, 'a couple of grazed knuckles.' She put her hands on the table and inspected them ruefully. 'But my hands were never my best asset.'

They certainly weren't soft with long painted nails like others he knew, he reflected, and paused suddenly on the thought.

'A bit disgraceful, aren't they?' she said with a chuckle, catching his suddenly narrowed look.

'Uh...no. I wasn't thinking that,' he confessed.

'What were you thinking?' she asked.

'I was thinking...that they're a good shape and I'm sure short nails are a good idea for the kind of life you lead and—that they're strong, capable hands.'

'Liar,' she said but with a twinkle in her eye. 'Are you going to make the cocoa or shall I?'

He said nothing for a moment and there was something both quizzical and enigmatic in his eyes. Then he said, 'Can you read my mind, Olivia?'

'In this instance, yes. I got the strong feeling you were thinking something quite different.'

'You're right,' he said slowly, and turned away to make the cocoa.

'Now, Ben, when I did something similar to you, you threatened to get all hot and bothered if I didn't *tell* you.'

He shrugged but said nothing until two steaming mugs were on the table in front of them. 'I was thinking—' he pulled out a chair and sat down '—that my remarks on feminine foibles were not only superior but quite unwarranted in your case and I'm only surprised you didn't take greater offence.'

She wrapped her hands around her mug and eyed him.

'You don't believe me?'

'Not entirely.'

'You're right.' He grinned. 'Well, not entirely right. I was actually thinking you're unlike most of the women of my acquaintance so it was the same thing *really*.'

'Unless you were thinking of one particular woman of your acquaintance,' she said after a little pause.

'My memory is still a bit patchy, I have to confess.'

Olivia stared at him. 'Are you *sure* you told the flying doctor this?'

'Yes. He said indiscriminate return of memory was quite usual.'

'I see. I must have been mad.'

He looked comically wary. 'Why?'

'To let you do what you did tonight, I—'

'Olivia.' He slid his hand across the table and covered hers. 'Don't worry so. I'll be OK.'

She hesitated but didn't draw her hand away. 'Your company will be worried about your plane.'

'There's not a lot that can be done at the moment.'

'No. I guess not.' She looked down at his hand still on hers then up into his eyes. 'I...I'm no further forward, Ben. Anyway, it's only a few hours since we...well...you know what I mean.'

He smiled slightly. 'I do. Because you can't make up your mind whether I'm the ultimate con man?'

A tinge of colour stained her cheeks. 'Wouldn't you have reservations if you were me?'

'Probably.' He raised his eyebrows. 'But then I'm not pressing you one way or the other.'

Olivia felt like saying that just sitting with her hand under his and in such close proximity, especially after they'd fought the elements and performed dangerous deeds together, was a form of pressure of its own. But she immediately decided that caution and discretion might serve her better.

As if he could see all this chasing through her grey eyes, Ben Bradshaw looked wry. He decided to change the subject and he took his hand away. 'Your roof needs a bit of work on it.'

Olivia sat back, not sure whether to be relieved or bereft. 'You're not wrong. In fact we need a whole new roof but it's such a large area.' She stopped and shrugged. 'I was hoping to be able to do it bit by bit but there are a lot of things that take precedence— fences, bores, pasture improvement and so on. Uncle Garth doesn't see a new roof as a priority either.'

Ben looked around the kitchen assessingly. 'That's a pity. The rest of the structure seems pretty sound.'

'It is,' Olivia said eagerly. 'They built these old brick walls to last. Do you know a lot about old buildings?'

He looked fleetingly surprised then smiled. 'I'm afraid I'm not as passionate about them as you are but then I can't boast a hundred-year association with anything. Well, I don't think I can.'

Olivia grimaced. 'Perhaps paranoia rather than passion would be more accurate but I can't seem to help it. Only…' She paused thoughtfully. 'I…no.'

'I think you should tell me,' he murmured.

'I'm sure you do,' she responded a shade tartly. 'You have a habit of insisting on knowing my innermost thoughts.'

'We are just the two of us stuck in a rising sea of water,' he observed mildly.

'Do you play cards?' she countered.

He looked amused. 'I seem to think I do but that can be a very boring way of passing the time, if that's what you had in mind.'

'It is. I'm beginning to feel as if I'm taking part in the Spanish Inquisition.'

He turned his mug around and drained his cocoa. 'On the other hand we seem to have agreed we have some sort of an effect on each other— I know.' He glinted her a wicked little look. 'We're not going to rush into anything, we're not even sure if there's anything to rush into! But we'll never know if we treat it all as a closed book. Will we?'

She looked at him frustratedly. 'It's not exactly a

two-way street, though. I know you can't help it at the moment but that's why I prefer to have a few reservations and prefer not to spill my whole soul to you, Mr Benedict Arnold.'

He narrowed his eyes. 'Let me guess, then. It's just occurred to you to wonder whether life might not be passing you by on account of your preoccupation with Wattle Creek and the hundred-year-old history of the Lockharts?'

Olivia bit her lip and pushed her fringe back with both hands.

He smiled slightly.

'That amuses you?' she queried dryly.

'No. It's the way you handle your hair. When you push your fringe aside it's, well, it's a unique little gesture that signifies something is really bothering you.'

'It needs a trim, that's all it signifies,' she said prosaically.

'Liar.' He said it softly but looked just as amused and incredulous as she had when she'd said it earlier.

Olivia coloured, looked exasperated then goaded. 'Oh, all right. It did cross my mind, that's all.'

'I think it's a very good thing that it has— No,' he drawled as she fired up to say something scathing, 'not from a self-interest point of view as you're about to accuse me of, I have no doubt, but because you have so much to offer, so much life to live here and now, it seems a shame for it to be passing you by.'

An acute feeling of annoyance gripped Olivia and her nostrils flared as her mouth hardened.

But he took the wind right out of her sails. 'You

should be lavishing all that wonderful spirit and creativity on a husband and children, my dear. Because I
think you could create a richness there that would be
quite something.'

Her lips parted and stayed parted until she closed
her mouth and swallowed visibly. 'You…you don't
know my uncle Garth by any chance?'

He raised an eyebrow. 'Why do you ask?'

'You could have taken the words right out of his
mouth!'

He grimaced. 'Sorry. I had no idea what his sentiments on the subject might be but I do know how
galling it can be to have people telling you what you
should do with your life—'

'It didn't seem to stop you from doing just that,'
she replied bitterly.

'Only in general,' he said slowly, and frowned. 'So
your uncle is getting a bit restive about Lockhart heirs
even by another name, Olivia?'

'He has some old-fashioned views,' she said acidly.
'If you're not barefoot, pregnant and tied to the
kitchen sink by the time you're twenty-one, you're
not much use to anyone in his estimation. He's convinced I'm on the shelf with only a dried-up spin-
sterhood in front of me.'

'Strange thinking for a bachelor,' Ben Bradshaw
commented.

'Not so strange. He got left at the altar, apparently—well, almost. Thrown over for another man at
least, which explains not only his bachelorhood but
his cynicism on the subject of women.'

'He must surely appreciate how good you are at helping to run the station, though?'

Olivia shrugged and sighed. 'Yes, he does. But it troubles him that I should be—so footloose and fancy-free.'

'Were.'

The single word dropped into a pool of silence apart from the rain drumming on the roof.

'Say that again?' She spoke ominously at last.

'I think you know what I mean, Olivia.' His lips twisted. 'For whatever reason, we're in a position where we find ourselves fancying each other something rotten not to be too finicky about our choice of words.'

She pushed her chair back precipitously and stood up.

He remained seated, entirely unperturbed, and looked up at her attentively.

'Well, I am finicky about my choice of words,' she stated fiercely.

He raised a lazy eyebrow at her. 'Whatever words you like to choose are not going to make it go away.'

'You're wrong, you know. Your choice of words has just banished any interest I may have thought I had in you, Mr Bradshaw. Sorry, but I'm like that.'

'Why don't you go to bed, Olivia?' he suggested.

'Who...how...who the hell do you think you are?'

'The man from the moon,' he agreed wryly. 'That doesn't prevent me from making a beneficial observation. You're tired, overwrought, cross enough to indulge in a fruitless discussion about semantics—and

I'm still extremely grateful for all you've done for me.'

Olivia stood stock-still, then, to compound her overwroughtness, heard herself make a sound of kittenish frustration that she would have scorned had it come from any other woman, so she did the only thing left for her to do. She swung on her heel and marched out. To return within a moment to say merely, 'You may sleep in the other spare bedroom.'

But Ben Bradshaw, with a fading smile on his face that he hadn't allowed her to see, remained at the kitchen table for a while longer, staring at nothing in particular because he was acutely aware that his life had suddenly become very complicated. I should really walk, or swim away right now, he reflected. Why should a bump on the head change—things? How could I remember most things but not the most important thing of all?

And what is it about her that attracts you? he asked himself. She's not the most beautiful girl in the world. She's independent to a fault, practical to a degree that makes you wonder if there's anything else to her— Ah, that's it. You're something of an enigma, Livvie Lockhart. And I can't deny that I'm intrigued. How much this has to do with temporary amnesia is another matter.

He got up at last, rinsed the mugs and took himself to a fresh, dry bed.

He was awoken the next morning by Ryan and Sonia and it was an unnerving experience to open his eyes and find himself staring into two pairs of identical round brown eyes set in freckled faces just level with his own.

'Hallelujah!' He sat up groggily. 'If it isn't the heavenly twins.'

They giggled. 'We just came to see how you were.'

'How very kind of you—did you have to use flippers?'

'No, silly,' Sonia said. 'It's stopped raining. But there are some lovely puddles out there. We left our wellies outside,' she added hastily.

'Why've you changed your room?' Ryan asked interestedly as he leant against the side of the high bed.

'The roof leaked all over my other one. Is Olivia up and about?'

'She's out like a light. We looked in but we were as quiet as little mice. Weren't we, Son?'

'Yes. Think she's all right?' Sonia asked conversationally. 'It's not like Livvie to sleep late.'

Ben explained about the broken night they'd had on top of the night before.

'Well, would you like us to show you around a bit?' Ryan offered. 'Then she can really have a sleep-in.'

'How exceedingly nice of you,' Ben responded, and they giggled again.

'Have I said something funny?'

'You talk funny, that's all. You talk to us as if we're grown-up, doesn't he, Son?'

Sonia nodded vigorously.

'Well, why wouldn't I?' Ben murmured. 'You saved my life after all. Can you give me a minute to get dressed?'

* * *

Olivia drifted up through layers of sleep, opening and closing her eyes occasionally then sitting bolt upright as she realized the sun was shining. On top of this phenomenon, a glance at her bedside clock told her it was nine-thirty.

She blinked confusedly then it all came flooding back. She lay back with a heartfelt groan and wondered how on earth she was going to confront Ben Bradshaw this morning.

Consequently, she took her time dressing, in her cream and red checked shirt this morning with her usual khaki working trousers, and she made her bed and tidied her room meticulously. Then she sat down at the dressing table and trimmed her fringe. As she was tying her hair up in a loose knot she frowned. During all her activity she'd heard no sounds at all.

Sleeping in too, I guess, she mused, and braced herself to leave the sanctuary of her bedroom.

But there was no sign of him although she searched right through the house. And despite herself she couldn't help herself from starting to worry. Had he lapsed into amnesia again and gone walkabout? Had he developed blood poisoning through his stitches—why, oh, why had she allowed him to exert himself like that last night?

She had her hand on the kitchen phone to ring Jack when he strolled in through the back door.

She slammed the phone back in its cradle. 'Where the hell have you been?'

He paused then said deliberately, 'Good morning, Olivia. Yes, it is a lovely morning; still a lot of water about but—'

'You know what I mean!'

'I don't as a matter of fact.' He eyed her narrowly.

'I thought you must have lost your memory again or be having raving delusions because your stitches got infected or...or...don't you dare laugh!'

'I'm sorry.' He sobered. 'It didn't occur to me that you'd be worried. I got a visitation from Sonia and Ryan. They thought it might be a good idea to give me a little tour of the place.'

'Sonia and Ryan!'

'Uh-huh. We decided to let you sleep in.'

Her expression defied description for a long moment then she sat down at the kitchen table and said gloomily, 'Those two will give me grey hairs before long.'

'Not only you,' he said amusedly. 'I notice their father already has them.'

'So they just walked in and invited you?'

'They were staring at me from close range when I opened my eyes. I thought I was sharing heaven with two unangelic cherubs.'

Olivia tried not to but burst out laughing. She stood up, still chuckling, and went to the fridge. 'So? Did you enjoy your little tour?' She took out some eggs and bacon and a tomato.

'Well, I got down to the machinery shed and had a chat to Jack, Davo—who is pretty sure he'll have the satellite phone up and running soon—as well as the twins' father. They were of the opinion, incidentally, that by tomorrow morning, if there's no more rain, we should be able to get a four-wheel-drive vehicle out to the plane.'

Olivia placed some strips of bacon in the frying-pan and cut the tomato in half. She picked a banana out of the fruit basket and peeled it. 'What is Jack's opinion on the weather?'

'There's another low headed this way but he reckons it'll hold off for a couple of days.'

'Glory be.' She started to set the table.

'Not good news?'

'That could be all it would take to flood us right out.'

'There's still a lot of water lying about.' He pulled out a chair and sat down at the kitchen table. 'You must have some higher ground.'

'It's getting pretty overpopulated. Still, we'll do what we can do.'

'How about your neighbouring properties? I mean, could they help out temporarily?'

'Well, I think—' she turned the bacon over '—Naroo to the east would be in much the same position as we are. Campbell Downs does have some higher ground but it's just changed hands in rather sad circumstances. I—' she grimaced '—would hesitate to approach the new owners.'

He sat back and pushed his hands into his pockets. 'Why sad?' he asked with a frown.

Olivia cracked two eggs into the pan and added the tomato and banana. She turned to him and waved the long fork she had in her hand. 'It was a family concern, a bit like Wattle, but all sorts of pressures forced them to sell out to a multinational company. I believe they have beef properties in Argentina and so on.'

'You obviously don't approve.' He was still frowning.

She hesitated. 'I shouldn't be judgmental but these were people who battled and fought and went through the good times, yes, as well as the bad—I suppose what I don't approve of in principle is the impersonal nature of these giant companies and the fact that primary producers who are not giant companies—well, not many of the population realize what a tough job it is.'

'There's a saying about bookmakers—as in the betting kind—and farmers. The former never admit to winning and the latter never stop whingeing.'

Olivia turned back to the stove and basted the eggs. 'I hope you don't subscribe to that kind of trite and silly nonsense.'

'Otherwise I might find myself going breakfastless?' he hazarded with a grin.

She looked frustrated. 'Don't you agree that's how little people *understand*, though? Not that I know anything about bookmakers. By the way, if you want to make yourself useful you might make the toast.'

He got up obediently and put two slices of bread into the toaster. Then he set out knives and forks, salt and pepper, butter and handed her two plates.

A minute later they sat down to perfectly cooked bacon and eggs, fried tomato and banana.

'Mmm—' he sniffed appreciatively '—this looks wonderful.'

Olivia buttered a piece of toast. 'You haven't commented,' she remarked.

'Well, I can only comment in general.' But he ate

thoughtfully for a few moments before he said, 'Feeding this planet is becoming more and more of a task, Olivia. And that's why individuals are—battling these days.'

She looked at him with a trace of scorn. 'That's extremely general, Ben.'

'But perhaps more relevant than you may think, Olivia,' he countered with an acute little glance.

'You must admit quality and taste can suffer when things are done on a large scale. For example, take these lovely eggs you're eating right now. They're not from battery hens—their mums did actually get to range free.'

He looked wry but said, 'On the other hand, the milk millions of Australians are drinking with their tea or coffee right now is free from tuberculosis et cetera.'

'I suppose you're right,' she said with a sigh. 'But, whilst I agree that there have to be all sorts of checks and controls, I still feel quite strongly that a rural population of people who care about their land and their produce is a better way to go and that governments should see this.'

'Well spoken,' he murmured.

'But you don't agree?'

He finished his breakfast and placed his knife and fork side by side on his plate. 'I think it's becoming more complicated these days, that's all.'

Olivia clicked her tongue then stood up. 'Coffee, tea—? No, of course not. Milk or orange juice, then?'

'Orange juice, thanks,' he replied with a grin. 'I'm very relieved that you're talking to me this morning, by the way.'

She removed their plates, poured him a glass of juice, set the coffeepot on the stove and shrugged. 'I might not have been if I hadn't—got a fright about what might have happened to you.'

'Does that mean to say you look upon me as your responsibility, Olivia?' he queried idly.

'Only so far as your health goes,' she retorted.

He waited until the coffee bubbled and she returned to the table with a mug steaming aromatically, to say, 'I see you've cut your fringe.'

She blinked. 'Not all that much.'

'No,' he agreed. 'About half an inch.'

'What's it to you anyway?'

The long glance they exchanged was curiously charged, she found herself thinking, or it became so as it lengthened.

Then he said a touch dryly, 'I think you must know, Olivia.'

She moved restlessly but couldn't bring herself to look away. 'Have you remembered anything new today?'

'No,' he said.

She grimaced. 'Well, what would you like to do now?'

'What did you have in mind?'

'I'm going to clean up here, sort out your former bedroom, get someone up to fix the roof and then I'll go and see the state of play on Wattle Creek with my own eyes.' She got up and began to clear the table.

'On foot?'

'No, I'll be riding.'

'Could I come?'

She paused briefly then turned to the sink. 'That may be a bit energetic for you. How's your head?'

'I haven't had a look but I'm sure I could ride a quiet horse.'

'I'll make a decision when I've finished this.'

He watched her back as she began, vigorously, to wash up. Then he got up quietly, picked up a tea towel and started to dry the dishes.

They worked in complete silence for ten minutes, Olivia expressionlessly although she couldn't believe how unnerving it was to be so close to him as their bodies brushed accidentally a couple of times.

Or is it accidental? she wondered, the second time it happened, and shot him a grey and angry glance.

He raised an eyebrow and rather pointedly removed himself from the immediate area.

But she was still annoyed and said shortly, 'Would you mind getting the first-aid kit?'

'Roger, willco!' He strolled out of the kitchen, leaving Olivia to grind her teeth.

Nor was her mood improved when he hadn't returned by the time she'd finished all she wanted to do in the kitchen. She was just about to go in search of him when he returned with the kit, whistling softly.

'Took your time,' she commented.

'I put the damp mattress out to air and hung all the bedclothes on the line,' he replied sweetly.

'You're a housewife's dream,' she responded with some bitterness. 'No wonder you feel so sure you'd make a good husband.'

'Did I say that?'

'Don't you remember?' She stopped and stared at him.

He grinned wickedly. 'Yes. But it wasn't from that point of view that I made the comment.'

'No,' she agreed, 'it was because you actually like women and their little foibles don't drive you mad.'

'I see I shall have to guard my tongue,' he murmured. 'You have a photographic memory, Olivia.'

'No one could accuse you of that. OK, let's have a look at you.'

He sat down.

She removed the dressing and was gratified to see that the faint redness around the stitches had mostly disappeared. 'Looking good,' she murmured, and with deft fingers put a new dressing on. 'How's the bump on your head?'

He touched his fingers to the back of his head. 'Subsiding nicely, thank you.'

'And the scratches on your face are healing.' She subjected his face to a minute scrutiny which he bore with equanimity although, as their gazes locked, she could see the laughter lurking in the deep blue of his eyes.

She flushed and straightened. 'Well, it's up to you—to ride or not to ride.'

'I'd love a ride,' he said earnestly. 'I feel much in need of some decent exercise.'

'Let's go. I'll lend you a hat.'

An hour later they were saddled up, Olivia on a restive bay gelding, Ben on a black mare with white socks and wise, placid eyes.

They jogged along in silence for a while as she took in the state of the countryside. The sun was still shining although there were big white cloud domes building on the horizon. It was hot and the ground, where it wasn't covered with water, was steaming.

Olivia repositioned her broad-brimmed hat and felt the sweat trickle down her face as her shirt started to cling to her body.

She cast Ben a couple of sideways glances but he sat on the black mare with all the easy assurance of a born horseman and it was soon plain to be seen that she was responding most favourably to his light-as-silk touch on her mouth. Indeed, her eyes were losing that wise, world-weary air as she pricked up her ears and a certain spring came to her step.

And Olivia suddenly started to chuckle.

'What?' Ben enquired, drawing alongside her.

'You, that's what,' she answered, still smiling. 'Well, you and being out of the house and not soaked to the skin and being able to cast off all my earlier "mood".'

'I'm glad,' he said gravely, 'but why me?'

'I've got the feeling you're dynamite when it comes to the female of the species be they human or equine. By the look on her face, Bonnie—' she gestured to the mare '—hasn't enjoyed herself so much for years.'

'Ah. In that case, do you think we could up the pace a bit?'

'A gentle canter would be nice,' she agreed, and urged her horse forward.

They toured several paddocks, stopping once to help a calf that was bogged by means of attaching the rope

Olivia had on her saddle to it and her horse towing it out of the mire. She did the riding while Ben pushed from behind, getting himself liberally coated with mud at the same time. Then she showed him the horse paddock where he'd been found.

They dismounted and he grimaced down at the rock he'd hit his head on. 'I think I must have been already groggy from the landing. Because I still don't remember anything about this paddock.'

'I think you might have been. Otherwise you surely wouldn't have set off with no identification and no hat. But you do remember the landing?'

'I remember setting it down but that's about it. Phew! It's bloody hot, isn't it?'

'You're not wrong, and you're a mess.' She looked at Graham's jeans and patch-pocketed khaki bush shirt then grinned at him. 'But I might just have the perfect solution. Follow me.'

They mounted again and she led him to the banks of Wattle Creek. It was lined with huge old ghost gums and wattle trees that were alive with birds and the sandy bed, only a few days ago all but dry apart from some deeper holes, was now running almost to the top of its low, grassy banks.

Olivia jumped off and led her horse down to have a drink. Then she knotted his reins up and let him loose to pick the grass.

Ben did the same although he said, 'They won't go walkabout?'

'Not any horse I've trained. Now this is the best part.' She took off her hat and her boots and waded into the creek fully clothed. 'It's marvellous,' she called, sitting down in the water and scooping it over her face and hair. 'Just mind your stitches!'

'You're a genius, Olivia Lockhart, and blow my stitches!' He sank down beside her and they laughed together as the fresh, cool water ran off them although he didn't dunk his head, washing away the sweat and the mud, and the sheer act of not caring about clothes or anything was delightful.

She rested back on her hands and raised her face to the treetops that were dispensing dappled sunlight. 'This is one of my favourite spots on the whole place.' She closed her eyes.

'I can see why. It's magic.'

'Well, it's not always like this but there are a couple of holes that never dry up. And when the wild flowers come out and the wattles are in bloom it's even better.'

'An artist's paradise?' He looked around at the gnarled white trunks of the gums.

'Yep!' She opened her eyes, sat up and pushed her fringe out of her eyes.

'I'm glad,' he murmured.

'That it's an artist's paradise?'

'That too but I'm glad you didn't cut your fringe too short.'

She opened her mouth then hesitated and, in a reflexive gesture, scooped more water over her head.

He said nothing and made no move but his eyes lingered on the wet tendrils of hair framing her face then his gaze wandered down to the outline of her figure beneath the wet shirt.

She moved uncomfortably, and he looked away.

But that was no good either, she discovered. It didn't lessen the sudden tension she felt; it heightened it if anything because, unlike him, she seemed to be powerless to remove her gaze from him.

'Olivia,' he said very quietly, and she jumped as he looked back into her eyes. 'You're right; it might not be a good idea.'

She blinked and looked at her hands under the clear running water. 'You think you can read *my* mind, Ben?'

'I think to be wet and cool and in this wonderful spot is adding to the awareness of each other that we've been battling one way or another all morning. If we're to be honest.'

She looked up and detected a glint of irony in his eyes, and was moved to irony herself, she discovered. 'Honest?' She smiled unamusedly. 'If that's what you want I can honestly tell you that I could think of nothing nicer than taking off all my clothes, although I have no intention of doing it, and having a proper swim. With you.'

'That's exceedingly honest. It so happens I'm of the same mind but I'm also the one who suffers from your extreme militancy when you stop and think that you don't know me from a bar of soap.'

'You bastard,' she whispered, and jumped up and deliberately kicked water all over him. Then she swung round and started to wade to the bank.

But he was impervious to the splashing she'd given him and he caught her before she made it.

'Don't,' she warned through her teeth.

'Relax, Olivia,' he drawled. 'All I'm going to do is kiss you.'

'Oh, no, you're not!'

He held her easily in his arms and for a moment there was something dark and satanic about him. Then it was gone, although he didn't let her go. But he did say, 'After that little image you created, it's the least I can do, and the least you can get away with, Olivia Lockhart.'

CHAPTER FOUR

'I'VE changed my mind,' she shot at him.

'No, you haven't,' he murmured. 'You're feeling a bit foolish and wishing you'd never said it but look upon it like this.' He raised a wry eyebrow at her. 'It could sort things out once and for all.'

'What do you mean?'

'Well, if you don't like the way I kiss you or vice versa, we can part as friends.'

'Oh!' she groaned. 'I really don't know why I put up with you, and after all I've done for you—'

He stopped the flow of her words in a time-honoured manner. He simply started to kiss her. And he did it in a way that she should have expected but did not. He kissed her lips lightly and told her she tasted of Wattle Creek but that it was delicious.

She twisted in his arms but he bent his head lower and kissed her neck and told her that it was a particularly slender, creamy, elegant neck and that it had taken to invading his dreams.

She put her hands behind her to try to force his apart but he murmured that she had a lovely, lithe figure, and, moving his hands down to her hips, commented that he was also much attracted to her rear and he guessed that so much riding was the reason for its compact, trim jauntiness.

She gasped with a mixture of annoyance and the

effect those wandering hands were having on her equilibrium and told him, tartly, to mind his own business.

He laughed softly at her and pulled her into an almost affectionate embrace, kissed the tip of her nose and said wickedly that he wished she would tell him how.

'You...you're playing with me!' she accused suddenly.

'Not in the least,' he denied with a straight face that didn't fool her for a moment.

'Yes, you are! You're no more serious than the man in the moon! Don't tell me this is how you kiss girls you are serious about.' She bit her lip as soon as the words left her mouth and blushed brilliantly.

'Ah.' He released her but took her wrist and touched his free fingers to her lips. 'Now that—*could* be a different matter.'

'I'm sure it could!' She tossed her head. 'I'm—'

'Olivia,' he broke in, 'before you invest me with all the sins known to Adam, if I have one golden rule, it's this. I don't go around kissing unwilling girls.'

'A moment ago you told me I wasn't unwilling,' she protested, and saw the trap too late.

His lips twisted. 'But then, Miss Lockhart, it's not really for me to say, is it? Not only from the point of view of my own little rule but I'm sure your spirit of sheer independence would agree.'

'So, unless I assure you I am willing—'

'That's it in a nutshell,' he agreed.

'You must think I came down with the last shower,' she retorted bitterly.

'All right,' he replied with a sudden narrowing of

his eyes, 'here's what we could do.' He released her wrist but didn't step away. 'If you don't want to be taken seriously all you have to do is—beat whatever kind of a retreat you deem worthy of the situation. Dignified, outraged—' he looked faintly amused '—it's up to you. If you decide to stay, however, then I would deem you willing.'

Her lips parted incredulously. 'And you expect me to believe that's not still a game of some sort?'

'I'm afraid you're going to have to try me, Olivia,' he drawled. 'But may I point out that the confusion that exists between us is this—do you want to be taken seriously or not?'

She suffered, she was later to think, a stunning but quite mad seizure of the brain. Prompted, no doubt, by his sheer effrontery and because she was immensely needled to think that he was virtually saying he could take it or leave it. That he could be serious or not, in other words.

'I've never kissed a man unseriously in my life,' she murmured, and shrugged. 'Must be the way I'm built. Sorry to be such a mass of contradictions, Ben Bradshaw, but I think I'll pass.' She gazed at him ingenuously. 'Just in case *you* get more than you bargained for.'

'Now that is laying down the gauntlet, Olivia.' His blue eyes were amused but there was something else in their depths that she couldn't quite identify—or so she thought, but almost immediately found she could. A cool little challenge glinted out of them.

'It's up to you.' Her own gaze was suddenly cool and challenging.

'Never let it be said I didn't seize the moment,' he said satirically.

'Or that you're ever lost for a word,' she commented dryly.

But the air between them was suddenly taut with a different kind of tension. Gone were the games—not that she had been playing games until she'd suffered that extraordinary seizure. Yet gone also was any semblance of friendship. It was as if a kind of hostility threaded the air, woven through with a dynamic streak of naked desire.

She couldn't doubt that the way his gaze was roaming down her was peculiarly intent and intimate. It was as if her body, moulded beneath her wet clothes, was taking shape in his mind without the impediment of any clothing. And it caused her to shiver, but not with cold. It was as if there was an electric current running through her.

It amazed her that with no physical contact between them she could feel this way but that didn't prevent her from, honestly and proudly, giving as good as she got, in a manner of speaking.

Quite candidly, she returned his scrutiny. She allowed her gaze to linger on the wide line of his shoulders then travel down his tall, sleek body as she remembered that, while he might not carry an ounce of extra flesh, he'd proved himself to be both strong and agile on the roof the night before—surprisingly strong.

But of course it wasn't only his body that attracted her, she thought; he had a personality that was almost impossible to resist. It was the way he made her laugh, when he wasn't incensing her, it was... She turned off her thoughts and closed her eyes briefly.

Then, without her quite knowing why she wasn't resisting, they were holding hands and only moments later, after one searching glance, she was in his arms being kissed in a way that wasn't at all playful but very adult and extremely arousing.

It was glorious, she found, to feel him touch her breasts or her hips, it was sensational to experience the quivers of desire that ran in waves down her as they kissed deeply and their bodies pressed together— it was lovely the way he initiated moments of respite that were curiously tender.

It was unique to be able to stretch her arms above her head and have him run his hands down her body then claim her mouth as she lowered her hands to his shoulders and felt herself gathered in against the hardness and strength of him.

And she didn't resist when he pushed aside the collar of her shirt so he could kiss the base of her throat; she curved her hands around his neck and tipped her head back to give him freer access. Then she cupped his face and indicated that she desired his mouth on hers again.

He obliged until she thought she might faint from the sheer pleasure of it.

It was the horses that brought them out of it.

Bonnie suddenly tossed her head, harrumphed and wandered down to the water's edge beside them to drink noisily, causing the birds in the tree to rise skittishly then settle with much clucking.

They broke apart although Ben immediately put his hands on her waist to steady her, and kept them there.

'Oh,' Olivia said breathlessly.

'A timely interruption?' he murmured, raising a wry eyebrow.

Olivia blinked then pulled herself away and sat down in the water and scooped it over her hair and face. He sat down as well and said after a moment, 'You were right.'

'How so?' It came out a bit unsteadily.

'That I might get more than I bargained for.'

She wiped water from her eyes and squeezed out her hair.

'No comment?' he remarked.

'None that I can think of at the moment.' She stood up and waded out of the creek.

He remained seated in the water, resting back on his hands, and watched as she tried to push the water out of her khaki trousers. 'I don't think we can just leave it at that,' he said presently as she pulled her boots on.

'Well, I do,' she muttered, and looked around for her hat.

He stood up at last. 'Are you of the opinion that it speaks for itself?' he queried with a trace of amusement. 'If so, I have to agree. Mere words would be quite inadequate to describe it.'

'I'm not proposing to describe it.' She clicked her tongue and whistled softly. Her horse trotted up obediently, and Bonnie stepped into the creek and put her nose against Ben's chest and blew softly down her nostrils.

Olivia's lips twitched. 'Anyone would think she was a chaperon but if Bonnie believes it's time to go so do I,' she said wryly, and swung herself up into the saddle.

Ben ploughed through the creek followed by Bonnie, who waited patiently for him to put his boots and hat on, then accepted his weight.

They rode side by side out of the fresh, green-dappled world of the creek into the harsh sunlight and within minutes their clothes were starting to dry on their backs.

'I have to *think* about this,' Olivia said at last. 'It's no good expecting me to— I mean to say I'm not some shy virgin you can expect to be totally bowled over.'

'I'm not some shy virgin either,' he said, 'but I was pretty close to being bowled over myself.'

'I find that hard to believe.'

'I know. There's a lot you find hard to believe about me but in fact the feeling is mutual right at this moment.'

'Really? I thought I was an open book to you, Ben Bradshaw.' She tossed him a bitter little look.

He shrugged. 'That was before you kissed me in a way that, had Bonnie not intervened, could have ended up—who knows where?'

Olivia drew an unsteady breath but straightened her spine. 'If you're telling me I've passed some sort of a test—'

'I didn't say that at all,' he objected. 'But since you brought it up, did I? Pass the test, I mean?'

She clenched her teeth then decided to be honest.

'Most admirably—as you damn well know. How—I mean—what kind of a test it *was* is something I still have to decide.'

'Do enlighten me,' he invited gravely.

She shot him a grey glance loaded with irony but managed to say serenely, 'Well, we have no way of knowing whether it's a kind of stock-in-trade of yours, do we?'

'You think I might have left a trail of women languishing around the countryside? I really don't think I'm that kind of man,' he said pensively.

'I know. If anything, you think you're God's gift to women, but you don't know me very well,' she pointed out.

'As a matter of fact I knew I wanted to kiss you when you were doing your Florence Nightingale bit for the first time.'

'All right,' Olivia said unamusedly, 'let's not go into that. Let's not go into *anything* until I've had a chance to think a bit. You know, this really couldn't have come at a worse time!' She looked around frustratedly then up at the sky. 'There's so much to do, the last thing I need on my mind is the question of whether you're a charming philanderer!'

He burst out laughing. 'I'm so sorry, Miss Lockhart. I shall endeavour not to—get in your way for the next few hours.'

She cast him a sceptical look as they trotted up to the stables.

In fact she didn't see him again until that evening.

Jack decided they'd be able to get to the plane in

the Land Rover and took him off.

She was making dinner when he walked into the kitchen carrying a briefcase. It was dark, and although not raining, heavy clouds had obscured the sunset.

'You obviously found it,' she said, taking in the briefcase.

'Mmm...' He hung his borrowed hat on the stand by the door, and looked stiff and weary, she thought.

'Why don't you freshen up?' she suggested. 'Then I might shout you a beer.'

He rolled his eyes appreciatively then looked down at himself ruefully. 'The only problem is that I haven't got anything else to wear, but these clothes do feel as if they've been cast in concrete on me.'

'Wear Graham's pyjamas,' she recommended briskly, and, at the sudden little look he shot her, added, 'Don't worry, I'm in Florence Nightingale mode, I shall be able to survive you in pyjamas.'

'What a pity,' he murmured, but went away immediately, with his briefcase.

Jack poked his head around the kitchen door a moment later.

'Come in,' Olivia said warmly. 'Like a beer?'

'Love one.' He put a case that contained the satellite phone on the table. 'Davo fixed it. Found the plane,' he added, and glanced around.

'He's getting washed and changed.' Olivia handed him a stubby and poured herself a glass of wine which she sipped while she stirred the spaghetti Bolognese she was preparing.

'He's lucky to be alive and he must be a hell of a

pilot. He remembers now having to glide the plane down with no power and miss not a few obstacles in the process, like trees and rocks. Excepting for the last rock which crumpled the nose wheel.' Jack grimaced. 'Would have given him a bit of a jolt too. Then he walked six miles to the horse paddock. I guess that explains why no one heard or saw anything.'

Olivia pulled out a chair and sat down with a frown. 'Does he remember anything more about himself? I mean, why he was on his way to Campbell Downs, what he does for this pastoral company he works for? His memory is coming back in patches, apparently, which the flying doctor told him is normal, but...' She stopped and gestured frustratedly.

'I'd say he's pretty high up in it,' Jack said slowly. 'He seems to know what he's talking about in relation to stock and that kind of thing and—I get the feeling he's a pretty cool customer. There's a bit of reserve about him that may not be entirely due to his lack of memory.'

Olivia absorbed this then said, 'Well, now we're not quite so flood-bound, unless it rains tonight, surely either his company or his family will come and retrieve him tomorrow?'

Jack finished his beer and stood up. 'Got to go. As for him, I'd say they could have got him any time they liked. All they'd need is a chopper. See you in the morning, Livvie.'

Why didn't I think of that? Olivia pondered as she got up to stir the sauce again and stand the spaghetti in a pot of boiling water. She inspected the salad she'd made and put it on the table as well as a bowl of parmesan cheese. She'd made a cheesecake for dessert and she topped it artistically with fruit salad.

Then she sat down again with her wine and was deep in thought when Ben arrived, clean, brushed and wearing not Graham's pyjamas but his khaki boiler suit which she'd washed and hung out but forgotten about.

'Oh.'

'May I?' he said, and pointed to the fridge.

'Of course.'

He got himself a beer and cracked the top off it but unlike Jack, who'd drunk straight from the bottle, he took a tall glass from the dresser and poured the foaming amber liquid into it.

Then he sat down and raised the glass to her. 'Cheers.'

'Cheers. I'd forgotten about your suit.'

'So had I. But I not only feel better dressed, I feel more modest.' He took a long draught of cold beer and she watched the muscles of his throat work as it slipped down.

'Jack said you performed a minor miracle getting your plane down.'

He shrugged. 'I think luck was on my side more than anything else.'

'What will you do with it?'

'That is very problematical, Olivia. Even fully operational it would be difficult to fly it out of that paddock and although it's only a four-seater getting a low-loader or something big enough in to load it onto and haul it out is going to take some doing. But I'm bending my mind to it.'

She was silent for a time and she got up to check the spaghetti. 'Tell me more about this pastoral company and why they haven't sent a helicopter up to rescue you, Ben,' she said presently as she drained the spaghetti and poured the sauce onto it.

He grimaced. 'They probably thought I was safe enough here and they've probably loaned their helicopter out to the emergency services. I would imagine there are those much more in need of rescue than I am with all this water about.'

Olivia considered this then nodded her head in agreement. 'I guess so. Well, tuck in.' She put the steaming platter of spaghetti Bolognese on the table and sat down again but added, 'Who are they?'

'The company? You may not have heard of them, they're new in the area.'

'I'd still like to know—' She paused as the phone rang. It was her uncle calling from Tokyo.

'Uncle Garth,' she said delightedly, and for the next five minutes documented the state of Wattle Creek minutely for him, made a few notes and finally assured him that he need not dash home because if anything could be done if more rain fell she and Jack were quite capable of doing it.

But as soon as she put the phone down she looked annoyed with herself. She resumed her seat and picked up her fork. 'I forgot to tell him about you.'

'So I heard,' he said ruefully. 'What do you think he would have advised you to do?'

'Put a halter and a leg rope on you.'

He looked comically taken aback. 'You're not serious, Olivia?'

'Until he had a good chance to inspect you, probe through your background, your credit rating, the state of your teeth, et cetera—yes, I am.'

'Are you saying,' he said slowly and looking arrested as he wound some spaghetti around his fork, 'that he vets every eligible man who crosses your path?'

'Not so much that, it doesn't usually get to that stage—but he's not above subtly pointing out to me when he considers they *might* be eligible.'

'How...uncomfortable,' Ben Bradshaw remarked.

'Oh, I'm used to it,' Olivia replied blithely.

'So—are you going to?'

She leant back in her chair and surveyed him seriously. 'Put a halter on you, Ben? No. I've got the feeling it might be like trying to capture the wind, anyway.'

'Is this feeling the product of some serious thinking you've done over the last few hours?' he asked with a suddenly acute little look.

She raised an eyebrow and twirled her wineglass. 'It's just—a feeling I have. It's nothing calculated from what I know because, of course, there's so little I know. So, just—intuition perhaps, Ben?'

'I don't like the sound of that,' he murmured, and pushed his plate away. 'Thank you, by the way; that was delicious.'

'What do you mean you don't like the sound of it?' Olivia asked irritably as she got up, removed the remains of the meal and brought out the cheesecake.

'There's nothing you can do about it. Because even if you remembered every last detail of your life I still think I might...be right.'

'Well, I don't think it's wise to convict me on something as ephemeral as that, Olivia. Now, if you suffered the conviction that we wouldn't suit in bed, yes, I'd agree there was nothing more to talk about.'

She flinched inwardly but made no comment. Instead she handed him the cream courteously.

'Thank you so much,' he drawled with a glint of wicked irony, and put a large dollop onto his cheese-cake.

She put the cream bowl down with a thud and glared at him with her hands on her hips.

'Olivia,' he said softly, 'we came so close to it earlier today, and don't tell me it wasn't what you wanted as much as I did; how can we ignore it?'

As if to emphasize this, he looked her up and down critically. She'd changed into a denim skirt that swirled around her legs and a short-sleeved, silky-knit grey jumper. Her hair was in its usual loose knot with some tendrils escaping down her neck, and the kitchen light glinted through them, making them ethereally fair. The skin of her arms was also fair and smooth.

And he said suddenly, 'You're a marvel, you know. I've seen girls who live and work in the city who are more tanned than you are.'

She took a breath, sat down again and managed to say prosaically, 'I told you, I have no ambition to become a dried-up old prune. I always wear long sleeves and a hat when I'm out and about as well as sunscreen. Perhaps I'm merely vain,' she added with a twist of her lips.

'Not in the accepted sense. But if you are about this I'm glad.'

It affected her curiously because it was said rather gently. She frowned and stared at him then smiled ruefully. 'Ben, I've got the feeling you might just *be* God's gift to women; you seem to know all the right things to say and all the right buttons to push but—'

'I could say the same for you.'

She paused and felt a slow tide of colour mount to her cheeks.

'I mean to say, you were pushing a few of the right buttons yourself earlier today.' He stared at her.

The colour settled in her cheeks and refused to go away, to her considerable embarrassment. Because, unfortunately, she couldn't rid her mind of a very clear recollection of the way she'd kissed Ben Bradshaw earlier in the day.

'Could you just be God's gift to men, Olivia?' he queried. 'That was a very—sexy—encounter.'

It was her sense of humour that came to her rescue, eventually. The thought of Bonnie intervening intruded on the hot memories she was experiencing. But the subsequent thought that it might have been Ben Bonnie had sought to claim for another delightful ride in the hands of a master horseman rather than anything else caused Olivia's lips to curve then she started to chuckle.

He looked at her quizzically. 'Going to let me in on the joke?'

Olivia rose. 'I think I may be small-time compared

to you in the matter of expertise, Ben, that's all. But I'll tell you something: whether you do go around breaking hearts or not, you have a lot of style and I should feel the poorer for not having known you.' She turned to the sink.

'Just a minute, Olivia,' he said in a voice she didn't recognize—cool and abrupt.

She turned and blinked in surprise.

He stood up and pushed his chair in neatly then leant his hands on the back. 'You don't think your reserve has something to do with the fact that you may not find me as easy to push, order around and manipulate as you would like?'

She gasped.

He raised an eyebrow at her with some cynicism.

'No...'

'Then why are you going out of your way to treat me like a recalcitrant youth?'

'I am not!'

'Could have fooled me,' he drawled.

'Perhaps the boot is on the other foot,' she shot back. 'Are you having trouble pushing, ordering me around and manipulating *me*?'

'Oh, I don't think so,' he said with a faint under-current of sarcasm. 'Anyway, my idea of being attracted to someone doesn't involve a duel for dominance.'

'That is the worst thing you could have said to me, Ben Bradshaw,' she said through lips white with anger.

'Because it's true?' he queried with soft satire.

'Because it couldn't be further from the truth,' she stated, and strode out of the kitchen.

She went to her studio, raging inwardly, and paced around for about five minutes as she examined the turmoil of emotions surging through her.

Uppermost, she discovered, was a sense of sheer incredulity that she could have got herself into this situation with a man she barely knew. But nearly as impossible, she thought, was what he expected of her under such conditions.

The darkest thought of all, however, was how easy it would be literally to be bowled over by Ben Bradshaw.

She paused in front of one of the easels, and, with a sudden decisiveness, turned the page with the galahs over the back of the sketch book and stared at the blank, new page revealed.

Then she hooked over a stool from the table with her foot, took up a pencil and started to sketch with no clear idea of what she wanted to draw but a compulsion to not only draw but ease her feeling of being knocked right off base, and to still the insidious little whisper in her mind that was asking her just how independent and dominating she was.

It was Wattle Creek that emerged as her pencil flew. First the ghost gums with their old, gnarled and knotted trunks in some detail and birds sitting along the branches that reached out over the water. Then the creek itself and the bushes along the bank, and finally, in the creek, a horse nuzzling a man—Bonnie and Ben.

Why this scene? she asked herself painfully as she

sat back at last. But at the same time she knew she'd captured it well and that it would make a lovely card because there was a warmth that came through between horse and man.

And she knew that it was much better, from an artistic point of view, to draw a scene that had captured your imagination than to set out to put on paper or canvas something that sent no sensory messages from your mind to your fingers.

All the same, as she studied it, she knew she'd resolved nothing in this frenzy of creativity.

She chewed the end of her pencil and someone knocked on the door.

'Come in!' she called without thinking, quite sure it had to be Jack or someone from the station, and she stuck her pencil behind her ear and rose. But it was Ben.

Ben with a tray and a coffee plunger and cups on it.

She closed her mouth and stared guardedly across the room at him.

'I've come to apologize,' he said quietly, setting the tray on the table.

'I—' she glanced from him to the tray and back again '—thought you didn't drink coffee?' And winced because it sounded not only inane but feeble.

'I made myself some cocoa. It's in the jug.' He pointed. 'But I made you some of the stuff I found in the fridge. Taking great care to follow the instructions on the tin to a T,' he added. 'Given my inexperience with coffee. I'm supposed to plunge this now, I be-

GET FREE BOOKS and a FREE GIFT
WHEN YOU PLAY THE...

Just scratch off the silver box with a coin. Then check below to see the gifts you get!

SLOT MACHINE GAME!

YES! I have scratched off the silver box. Please send me the 2 free books and gift for which I qualify. I understand I am under no obligation to purchase any books, as explained on the back of this card.

306 HDL C4GH

106 HDL C4F7
(H-P-OS-08/00)

NAME (PLEASE PRINT CLEARLY)

ADDRESS

APT.#   CITY

STATE/PROV.   ZIP/POSTAL CODE

7	7	7	**Worth TWO FREE BOOKS plus a BONUS Mystery Gift!**
🍒	🍒	🍒	**Worth TWO FREE BOOKS!**
♣	♣	♣	**Worth ONE FREE BOOK!**
🔔	🔔	🍒	**TRY AGAIN!**

Offer limited to one per household and not valid to current Harlequin Presents® subscribers. All orders subject to approval.

© 2000 HARLEQUIN ENTERPRISES LTD. ® and TM are trademarks owned by Harlequin Enterprises Ltd.

DETACH AND MAIL CARD TODAY!

The Harlequin Reader Service® — Here's how it works:

Accepting your 2 free books and gift places you under no obligation to buy anything. You may keep the books and gift and return the shipping statement marked "cancel." If you do not cancel, about a month later we'll send you 6 additional novels and bill you just $3.34 each in the U.S., or $3.74 each in Canada, plus 25¢ shipping & handling per book and applicable taxes if any.* That's the complete price and — compared to cover prices of $3.99 each in the U.S. and $4.50 each in Canada — it's quite a bargain! You may cancel at any time, but if you choose to continue, every month we'll send you 6 more books, which you may either purchase at the discount price or return to us and cancel your subscription.

*Terms and prices subject to change without notice. Sales tax applicable in N.Y. Canadian residents will be charged applicable provincial taxes and GST.

If offer card is missing write to: Harlequin Reader Service, 3010 Walden Ave., P.O. Box 1867, Buffalo NY 14240-1867

BUSINESS REPLY MAIL
FIRST-CLASS MAIL   PERMIT NO. 717   BUFFALO, NY

POSTAGE WILL BE PAID BY ADDRESSEE

HARLEQUIN READER SERVICE
3010 WALDEN AVE
PO BOX 1867
BUFFALO NY 14240-9952

NO POSTAGE
NECESSARY
IF MAILED
IN THE
UNITED STATES

lieve.' He pushed the plunger down with the palm of his hand and a serious expression.

'You're impossible, you know,' she said.

'Because I want to apologize? I should have thought that might make me the opposite,' he replied with a lurking little smile.

'No. Because you—I don't know, cut the ground from under my feet at times.'

'I thought you were going to say because I could be very nice, at times.' There was a wicked little glint in his eyes.

'I still haven't forgotten what you said.' But although she tossed her head on this statement her words seemed to lack any severity.

He poured the coffee, then the cocoa, and handed her her cup. 'I suppose I was a bit cut to the quick,' he murmured wryly. 'I mean, what you said to me was fairly damning. To be honest, I don't think I've ever been damned with such faint praise before in my life.'

'What you can remember of it,' Olivia said a shade dryly. 'It doesn't appear to have actually damned you that much,' she observed.

'Did you expect me to throw myself off the roof?' He shot her a very blue, laughing glance.

'No. But then don't expect me to be taken in either, Ben.'

He considered for a moment. 'All right. But I was—bloody annoyed at the time. Oh!' His gaze came to rest on her sketch. 'Did you just do this?'

'Yes.' It was a reluctant monosyllable she produced. Then she remembered the pencil stuck behind her ear and drew it out.

'Does that—mean anything?' he asked as he studied the sketch critically.

Olivia sipped some coffee. 'Only that sometimes artists are compulsive and it was a—moving moment in a funny way.'

'I see,' he said neutrally.

'Would you like it?' What prompted her to say it, Olivia didn't know.

'As a memento of Wattle Creek once I'm irrevocably banished from it?'

She moved restlessly and sat down on a stool at the table. He pulled the other stool up and sat beside her.

'Olivia?'

'I just thought…' She shrugged. 'Bonnie was so taken with you, that's all.'

'I can't help feeling that, despite her best intentions, I would have been better off without Bonnie's devotion—if you're going to hold that against me as well.'

Olivia grimaced and was silent.

'What was I saying?' He frowned. 'Yes. I was certainly annoyed and therefore prompted to be a bit—unkind, perhaps.'

'I'd hate to think what you'd class as *very* unkind.'

He looked at her. 'I might have touched a sore spot.'

'I don't really think so. Look, I may be independent but I've never thought I was domineering, not in that regard.'

Their gazes locked. Until he said, 'Should we call a truce?'

Her lips parted.

'I mean so that we could each get a good night's sleep, which we deserve, don't we?'

'Just that?'

'Just that,' he repeated. 'You look as if you could do with it.'

'I feel as if I could do with it. But there are still the dishes to do and so on.'

'I don't know about the "so on" but the dishes are done.'

'Again? My gratitude is boundless,' she said with a slow smile growing in her eyes.

He put his arm around her shoulders and, after a slight tensing, she relaxed and didn't pull away. 'Are we friends?' he asked lightly.

She hesitated then gave in. 'Yes. Well—'

'Don't say it,' he warned. 'I get the message anyway. Go to bed, Livvie Lockhart. You've had a big day.' He took his arm away.

She stood up after a moment. 'You keep telling me that.'

He turned to her and said humorously, 'Could be that I know what's good for you.'

Olivia was seized by the desire to run her fingers down the angles and planes of his face, and to rest her lips lightly on his. But she contained herself and said, 'Could be that you talk too much, Benedict Arnold. Goodnight. Let's hope it is a peaceful night.'

* * *

She certainly slept deeply and peacefully and awoke to a splendid dawn. Gone were the clouds of the night before and the further threat of rain and it was cool and dewy with apricot fingers of light spreading from the horizon. It enticed her out onto the veranda to watch the sun rise. And as it did and the birds woke she went barefoot down into the revitalized garden, still in her pyjamas, and picked a bunch of flowers.

Then she stood still on the edge of the lawn and stared back at the house with its old bricks, the curved veranda roof, and the creepers that grew along it. At the comfortable wicker chairs and pot plants—and thought of how much it meant to her.

But then so did all of Wattle Creek, she reflected, and turned to look towards the horizon again. She leant against the fence that surrounded the garden plot, and could see for miles. All that sunburnt country in its early morning shades of pink, sienna and that startling sandy red that so amazed people and soaked up moisture so that even only twenty-four hours after a virtual deluge it appeared dry. And in an amazingly short time would be green again.

As she drank it all in, though, and felt a surge of elation flow through her veins, she knew unerringly that to see Wattle Creek Station looking beautiful was only a fillip and she buried her face suddenly in the flowers.

Because the main source of her feeling of well-being was still asleep—most probably—but she'd woken with Ben Bradshaw on her mind and it had filled her with a sense of anticipation and renewal to think of him—and that could mean only one thing.

I've fallen in love with him, she told the flowers silently. I know I shouldn't be, I know I barely know him and all the rest but I just can't help it. I couldn't feel so good otherwise, so…happy to think that he's still here and can make me laugh, make me ache with desire, make me want to sharpen my wits on him and occasionally fighting mad at him… Just so alive. It has to be that.

And to think that only last night I was so sure it couldn't be happening to me. Or perhaps *shouldn't* be happening to me. Then he charmed me right out of it…

'Of course, what I do about it is another matter,' she said barely audibly to the rising sun.

CHAPTER FIVE

AT THE same time, Ben Bradshaw, who was not asleep but standing unseen in the shadows cast by the curtains at his veranda door, watched as Olivia turned at last from the fence and walked back across the lawn with her bunch of flowers. She was obviously deep in thought.

What is going through your head now, my beautiful Livvie Lockhart? he wondered. And immediately felt a strange little jolt. Because only two nights ago you were telling yourself she wasn't the most beautiful girl in the world? he thought dryly. How things can change. But then, you didn't expect such a passionate Livvie Lockhart, did you? You didn't really expect to enjoy kissing her to the degree that you did.

Well, he amended to himself, what you didn't expect was that she would allow it to get as serious as it got because *you* had no intention of going to those lengths, did you? And with good reason. So why the hell did you go any lengths at all? Because this girl gets to you, he answered himself—and stared into the middle distance with a frown in his eyes.

A frown that was there for several reasons, not the least being how difficult it was going to be to come clean. The sooner the better, he told himself.

'Good morning.'

Olivia looked up. She was in the wash-house sorting the laundry. It was separate from the main house, set across the lawn from the kitchen beside the water tanks, and through the open doorway the resident guinea fowl were pecking at delicacies in the grass, their grey and white spotted feathers sleek, their blue heads and red combs extremely busy.

'Good morning,' she responded, a little shyly, he thought, and narrowed his eyes. But she went on immediately with more of her usual assurance. 'Thought you were still asleep! It's an—intoxicating kind of day.'

'I see that.' He stood in the doorway and looked outside. 'So the rains didn't come again— Do you ever eat them?'

Olivia blinked and drew her mind from the sheer pleasure of his company, the little things. The way his thick dark hair lay, how blue his eyes were, how tall he was in his khaki boiler suit. 'The guinea fowl? No, of course not.'

'But they are edible. I know of a farm in Victoria that's building quite a business out of them. Their meat is not only tasty but low-cholestrol and has virtually no fat. Apparently, the French are so taken with the taste of them about eighty million birds are consumed annually. Free-range game birds are considered a gourmet's delight. And I know free-ranging is close to your heart.'

Olivia had stooped to pick up some clothes and she straightened with a quizzical expression. 'It may be but no one is eating *my* guinea fowl. I just like to have them around. You seem to know an awful lot about them,' she added curiously. 'How come?'

He paused and shrugged. 'Perhaps I have a mind packed with trivia.' He paused again and saw the fleeting little look of frustration that came and went from her eyes. 'Actually,' he said slowly, 'it's my business to know these things.'

'What do you mean?'

'Walk with me for a little while, Olivia?' he suggested.

'I—' She looked around at the piles of laundry. 'Well—'

'You did say it was a wonderful day.'

'All right. I guess the washing can wait.'

So they walked to the garden fence and, at his suggestion, sat down on the grass beneath a flowering gum. She had on her denim skirt of the night before but with a primrose blouse this morning, and a pair of brown leather sandals. She'd washed her hair and it was shiny fair, full of life and escaping from its knot in curly tendrils.

'It's so lovely after rain, isn't it?' she said, looking around. 'You tend to forget that in a few weeks it'll be dry and dusty again. OK, why did you want me to walk with you? It sounded almost ominous,' she said ruefully, hugging her knees.

He leant back on his hands and stretched out his long legs. 'I don't think you'll approve, somehow, but, you see, I'm the chief executive of the company that bought Campbell Downs.'

'*What?*'

'I'm afraid so. And that's what I meant about it being my business to know these things—we don't only own grazing properties.'

Olivia could only stare at him speechlessly.

'I knew you wouldn't approve,' he murmured.

'I'm stunned,' she said. 'Do you just work for them or are you a multinational millionaire?'

'I don't know about that but it is my company. I'm the chief shareholder in other words.'

'No wonder,' she breathed, 'you didn't agree with me about— How long have you known this?'

He held her grey gaze steadily. 'It has been coming back in patches, my memory, but most of this came back as soon as the plane was mentioned.'

'And you didn't tell me? How could you?' She stared at him with clear hurt in her eyes.

'There…' he paused and grimaced '…was a reason for that.'

'I'll bet,' she said stiffly. 'Was it more convenient to have me thinking you were just the son of a blacksmith, Ben Bradshaw?' She looked at him bitterly. 'In case I got too attracted to your multinational, multimillions?'

'Not at all, Olivia. I am the son of a blacksmith who married a teacher. He's dead—my mother is still alive. But although he was a raw young man from the bush he turned out, with her help, to be wise and canny and between them they started to deal in rural real estate, she inherited a run-down property, and they made a small fortune. Things have gone on from there.'

'Why haven't I ever heard of you?'

'Because we are new in this area, but you must have heard of Pascoe Lyall. It's the operating name of the company that bought Campbell.'

Olivia crossed her legs and smoothed her skirt over them. Just over the fence, the grass wasn't mown and the stalks and seed heads were waving in a gentle breeze and filling the air with their fragrance. And the honey smell from the flowering gum tips above was wafting down. But, although she automatically registered it, it brought her no comfort.

'Yes, I've heard of Pascoe Lyall.' She shrugged.

'As a matter of fact, if it had continued to rain, I was going to offer you agistment on Campbell Downs.'

'How kind of you—am I going to have to drag the reason why you couldn't have told me this as soon as you remembered it out of you, Ben?'

He raised a wry eyebrow. 'You seemed to have enough good reason to—doubt me, as it was. So, when I heard your sentiments on the subject of impersonal, giant pastoral companies, I thought I might stay mum for a while. That was one reason anyway.'

'Coward,' she said with feeling. 'Why have you told me now?'

He looked away from her and she got the feeling he was suffering a moment of indecision. Then he said, 'Olivia, I think I should not impose on you any longer. I need to get back to work anyway and there are a couple of very complicated situations I need to sort out so...' He reached through the fence and pulled out a stalk of grass to chew. 'But, with your permission, this need not be goodbye.'

'There you are!' Jack arrived beside them puffing. 'Been scouring Wattle for the two of you. Ben, Davo's had a brainwave. Instead of trying to load your plane *onto* a truck, he's come up with a winch system so we can tow it behind. We can keep the nose up, play out the chain or haul it in as we need to. What do you reckon?'

'Just might work,' Ben said thoughtfully.

'They're still predicting rain although it don't look like it at the moment, and this might be the best opportunity we'll get for a while,' Jack added with some urgency. 'And if it can be repaired here you could fly it off from our airstrip.'

'Good thinking,' Ben said and stood up. 'Like to come, Olivia?' He held his hand down to her.

She took it after a slight hesitation and stood up but said quietly, 'No, thanks. I've got plenty to do here.'

He looked into her eyes searchingly but she looked away.

He said, slowly, 'There's a helicopter coming to pick me up this afternoon—I made a call this morning. Just in case we get delayed—'

'I'll let the pilot know what's happening. Off you go!' she said brightly.

She went back to the washing but in a daze.

I can't *think*, she castigated herself once. This morning I was sure I was in love with a man I knew nothing about because I couldn't seem to help myself and it didn't appear to matter a whit whether he was a blacksmith himself, not to mention a possible philanderer.

Now I know that he's anything but—well, that he's a man of substance if nothing else I...

She rubbed her face. I what? I just don't know what to think! And two things are at the root of it—in essence he's lied to me, and I *don't* approve of vast, impersonal companies like his because I know exactly how I'd feel if I had to walk off Wattle Creek. How does that change the man himself, though? The one who made me wake up this morning with such a light, expectant heart? The man it was such a joy to behold only an hour ago?

She forced herself to keep working—it was the day of the week she not only did the laundry but also cleaned the homestead. She hung the washing up as it came out of the machine and as the sheets, towels and table linen dried, with that lovely redolence of sunlight and fresh air, she vacuumed, polished and dusted. But all the time she felt jittery and uncertain.

There was no sign of the plane-rescue crew by lunchtime, so she cut herself some sandwiches and took a tea tray to the veranda. She'd just finished eating and was pouring herself a second cup of tea when she heard a faint buzzing that grew to the distinctive whipping sound of helicopter rotors at close range.

It had 'Pascoe Lyall' written in red on its white sides and it landed just beyond the garden gate.

She could see two people in it and one didn't wait for the rotors to stop, but jumped down and ran, bent low, through the cloud of dust being whipped up. It was a girl with long hair and wearing designer jeans, high-heeled boots and a white voile blouse.

Olivia stood up and started to walk across the lawn to meet her. At the same time she took in more details of this girl: sleek and shining dark hair that fell to below her shoulders, a pair of very expensive gold and tortoiseshell sunglasses that masked her eyes but didn't hide her glossy golden skin, and a pair of full red lips.

Her figure was little short of sensational and she had an undeniable air of assurance, long red nails that matched her lips, a gold watch and a gold link bracelet, little diamond studded hoops in her ears, and a large diamond on her left hand. She also looked vaguely familiar.

They met at the garden gate.

The girl said, 'Hi! This is Wattle Creek, isn't it?'

Olivia overcame a nameless feeling of dread to agree that it was.

The girl put out her hand. 'Then you must be Olivia Lockhart—how do you do? I'm Caitlin Foster, Ben's fiancée. I've come to take him home.'

It was a moment before Olivia could make her voice work. Then she said, 'Come in. Both of you.'

By this time the pilot had arrived at the gate, a middle-aged man in a pale blue shirt and navy trousers with the insignia of Pascoe Lyall—a P and an L twined together—on his pocket beneath a pair of wings.

He introduced himself as Steve Williams then looked around a shade warily, Olivia thought, as much as she was capable of thinking rationally as a cold rage started to possess her.

'Ben's not here at the moment,' she said, and explained about the plane. 'But please come in, I'll make you some tea or whatever you'd like. They've been gone for hours so I expect they won't be much longer.'

'What a marvellous old house,' Caitlin Foster enthused.

'Thank you. Tea, coffee or something cold?' Olivia asked as she led them into the lounge when she would normally have taken them through to the kitchen. Why? she wondered. Because my pride needs propping up?

'Something cold would be *luverly*,' Caitlin said, 'but don't go to any trouble. We're so grateful for all you've done for Ben as it is. How is he? I believe he actually lost his memory for a while.'

'Only selectively,' Olivia murmured.

'Selectively?' Caitlin raised an eyebrow.

'Well, he remembered bits and pieces, and it came back in bits and pieces—quite normal, the flying doctor assured us. I'll be right back. Do sit down.'

She was back in five minutes with a jug of lemon squash and two tall glasses. 'So, how long have you been engaged to Ben, Caitlin?'

'Six months.' She had slid her sunglasses up on top of her head and revealed a pair of sparkling dark eyes. 'I keep telling him it's time we tied the knot but between our various commitments—I'm an actress and a model—we never seem to find the time.'

'Oh,' Olivia said, suddenly enlightened. 'That's where I've seen you before.'

Steve spoke. 'I believe he had to have some stitches?'

'Yes, he cut his head but it's healing well—and here he is right now...' she paused as she heard a vehicle stop outside then start up again '...so he can tell you all about it himself.'

She stood up but not before she'd noticed that oddly wary look about Steve Williams again.

She frowned then turned to the doorway as footsteps made their way down the passage. 'We're in the lounge, Ben,' she called, and added to herself, You bastard!

He came in, started to stay, 'Mission acc—' and stopped abruptly as Caitlin got up and walked straight into his arms.

'Darling! I've being going out of my mind—why didn't you ring me?'

Ben Bradshaw looked down into Caitlin's vivid face and Olivia held her breath and prayed for some sign of shock or sheer surprise, some indication that this girl came as a complete and sudden revelation to him—and immediately asked herself why. Would it be easier to forgive the fact that he was engaged if he didn't remember it?

But a moment later he said with no surprise, 'Why, Caiti, how did you persuade Steve to bring you?' And he raised his dark blue eyes to the pilot over her shoulder with a clear, pointed question in them.

Steve looked as wary as he ever had and Olivia understood even before he said apologetically and uncomfortably, 'She just wouldn't take no for an answer, boss.'

'Why should I?' Caitlin asked spiritedly, and touched her fingertips to the dressing on Ben's temple. 'Now don't be cross, darling—and don't tell me you don't remember *me*!'

'Perish the thought,' Ben murmured, and kissed her lightly on the forehead. 'Well—' he looked up and across into Olivia's eyes '—may I join the party? I'm dying of thirst.'

'I'll get another glass,' Olivia said expressionlessly.

But after she'd delivered the glass and found that Steve had taken himself back to the helicopter she said brightly, 'I'll leave you two alone; you'll have some catching up to do. Give me a call when you're ready to go.'

She went straight to her studio and with shaking fingers reached for her sketch of Ben, Bonnie and the creek. But he must have virtually followed her out of the lounge because although she'd torn it off the pad she hadn't had time to tear it up when he opened the studio door, came in and closed it behind him. And walked straight over to her to close his hands over hers then prise the sketch gently out of them.

'Go away,' she said huskily. 'But just for the record, Ben Bradshaw, when *did* you remember her? From day one? Did you ever lose your memory for more than an hour or two?'

'Olivia—yes, I did,' he said quietly.

'But you didn't even look surprised,' she countered crisply.

'I wasn't,' he agreed. 'I had in fact remembered

Caitlin, curiously enough, the night we were discussing your hands after our escapade on the roof.'

She gasped. 'How can you stand there—?'

'It was quite strange how it came back,' he persisted evenly. 'It was the difference between your capable hands and her long, always red nails that first occurred to me, then it fell into place.'

'That's no defence,' she said incredulously after a moment. 'Once you remembered you had a fiancée you—you—' She couldn't get the words out, she discovered, and was horrified to find she had tears prickling her eyelids.

'We,' he said.

'Don't do that to me again, Benedict Arnold!' she said furiously and with unmistakable emphasis.

'But it's true. Even though it started because of temporary amnesia, it affected us both. I can remember thinking, that night, after you went to bed, how complicated my life had become. Because you see, Olivia, I can't pretend to myself that I should be marrying anyone when I'm attracted to someone else, even under the influence of amnesia.'

She laughed, a choked little sound that broke off in the middle. 'That's something I may have been able to forgive you for, curiously,' she said with supreme irony, 'but not this.'

'Why?'

She blinked at him. 'Do you really need me to tell you why? In essence you lied to me, twice, not only about being engaged but who you are. And I'm damn sure you hadn't proposed to tell me about Caitlin Foster either because the last thing you expected was for her to turn up here—your pilot has been looking all hangdog ever since they landed.'

'I was about to tell you when Jack turned up this morning.'

'That would also have been too late. But what did you propose to do with her, anyway? Break the engagement until you could decide how serious you might be about me?'

'I haven't had time to decide one way or the other, Olivia. I didn't *plan* any of this any more than I planned to have to crash-land in one of your paddocks.'

She drew a breath and turned away from him abruptly.

'Nor was I aware that it meant so much to you,' he added quietly. 'You were the one who told me you weren't some virgin—'

'I know what I said.' She sniffed and turned back to him. 'What have you done with her?'

'Caiti? She's waiting with Steve— Olivia...' He paused and frowned at the suspicious moisture on her lashes.

But she took no notice and took a hanky from her pocket to blow her nose and dab at her eyes. Then she picked up the sketch he'd dropped onto the table and said quite steadily, 'Take this with you, Ben. You won't be seeing Wattle Creek again. I'll walk you to the helicopter. Is there anything—? Your briefcase. We'll get that on the way through.' And she handed him the paper and walked to the door.

'Olivia.'

Her eyes were dry but not only that as she looked

back at him over her shoulder—they were suddenly ablaze with anger. 'There is no more to say, Ben Bradshaw. Let's go.'

He studied her for a long moment and once again she thought that he might be making up his mind about something. But he said at last, 'Say goodbye to Bonnie for me. And Sonia and Ryan.'

She didn't answer, and the faintest smile twisted his lips which should have warned her but didn't.

Because he crossed the couple of feet separating them, tilted her chin with his fingers and murmured, 'As to whether it's all been said, we shall see. In the meantime, look after yourself, Livvie Lockhart. You were a wonderful nurse.' And he kissed her gently.

'So that's about it,' Olivia said to her uncle Garth four days later.

Four days during which she had futilely examined every single thing she and Ben had said to each other, every nuance, and the little thought that he couldn't, as he'd said, have planned it all. But this thought was always followed by the same one—what difference did it make? He'd admitted he'd known about Caitlin when he'd kissed her in the creek...

'What happened to the plane?'

She came back to the present with a start to see her uncle staring at her. 'Well, they flew a mechanic in and a new nose wheel and flew the plane out. More importantly, as for the floods, we didn't lose any stock although it looked touch-and-go for a while. More rain would have caused a real problem.'

They were eating dinner in the kitchen. Garth

Lockhart had arrived home that afternoon looking unusually tired but Olivia had put it down to the rigours of jet lag and having to drive himself from Mackay to Wattle Creek.

She also knew she wasn't looking her best because over the last four days she'd found it difficult to sleep and eat and not only had she conducted that futile soliloquy with herself, she'd tried to bury her anger and sorrow under a punishing workload that had seen her in the saddle for hours on end.

She'd consoled herself with the thought that at least Wattle Creek had benefited. There was not a fence hole that had escaped her eagle eye. All the stock was where it should be and the preparations for the last muster of the season before it got too hot were well in hand.

Garth Lockhart pushed his plate of roast lamb away half-eaten and Olivia said contritely, 'Sorry. I should have made a lighter meal; you must be exhausted. But it is your favourite.'

'It's not that,' he said, and looked his niece over thoughtfully. He was a thick-set man, not very tall, with sparse grey hair and a red complexion. They shared the same grey eyes, uncle and niece, but the resemblance ended there. 'What did you think of him?'

'Who?'

'Ben Bradshaw.'

Olivia hesitated and ate a portion of roast pumpkin. Then she shrugged. 'I wasn't that taken with him as a matter of fact. Then I found out who he was and was less taken.'

'He's a good stamp of a man, though. And been to all the right schools. He's also a crackerjack polo player—spent a bit of time in Argentina, I believe. That's how he got so good at polo as well as picking up the odd ranch or two there.'

'Bully for him,' Olivia murmured. 'No wonder no horse is game to throw him.' She glanced at her uncle through her lashes and frowned faintly. 'He's *also* engaged to a simply stunning girl—do you remember Caitlin Foster? She was in that TV hospital series, amongst others.'

Garth folded his hands behind his head and appeared to ruminate.

'You weren't thinking along your usual lines of eligible men to marry me off to, by any chance?' Olivia asked wryly. She frowned again. 'But you don't even know him. Do you?'

'Livvie,' her uncle said heavily, and pulled his hands away to rest his arms on the table, 'yes, I do. I've met him, at least.'

Olivia stood up and began to clear the table but she stopped abruptly. *'What?'*

'No, don't worry, I wasn't thinking of marrying you off to him,' Garth said hastily. 'Although I really don't know why you haven't found yourself a man yet, Livvie—'

'Don't start that—just don't start,' she warned through her teeth, and began to pick up plates again.

Her uncle looked at her with some surprise and growing injury in his eyes. Then he sighed and said, 'Sit down, girl. I need to talk to you.'

Olivia hesitated then did as she was bid. 'So long

as you stay off men and Ben Bradshaw in particular,'
she said coolly.

'I—well, let me start at the beginning.' But he
stopped, rubbed his face and didn't seem to know how
to go on.

Olivia stared at him and finally said in a different
voice altogether, 'Something's wrong, Uncle Garth,
isn't it?' She put her hand over his. 'Please tell me,'
she added gently.

'Well, I didn't only go to Tokyo, Livvie. I went to
hospital and had some tests... Things don't look too
good, I'm afraid. I've got to have an operation but
even if it's a success—it's a heart and circulatory
problem, something to do with my carotid artery, you
see—I've got to take things easy for the rest of my
life.'

She closed her eyes then got up and put her arms
around him. 'Why—oh, why—didn't you tell me
sooner?' She hugged him close then kissed the top of
his head. 'But you'll pull through— How did you
manage to hide it from me?' she asked with sudden
guilt in her eyes as she pulled her chair round so she
could sit down beside him.

He looked shamefaced and it smote her heart to
think of this proud, normally pugnacious man looking
like that. 'I—well, the few times I felt really off I told
you—I made up stories that I'd strained my back and
so on. Then, a month ago, I went to see Doc Hayden
and he set up an appointment with a specialist on the
Coast. I knew then that I was in trouble but I insisted
on having more tests and some time to—organize
things.'

'You're an old fraud,' she said softly. 'You could have killed yourself! There's nothing to organize anyway. So you'll be having this operation just as soon as it can be arranged—and there's nothing more to say!' But she flinched inwardly as the words echoed in her mind and she remembered saying them in a different context four days ago.

'I'm afraid there is, Livvie. You see, that's how I came to meet Ben Bradshaw.'

'How?' She stared at him with her lips parted.

'Livvie—' Garth moved restlessly '—we couldn't go on, not now. It's been a battle anyway, for the last few years; you know that yourself. And there's no way you could cope—'

'I— What are you saying?' Olivia whispered, going dreadfully pale.

'I went to see him. I knew Wattle would interest him because it adjoins Campbell Downs. I...it's the only thing we can do, my dear.'

But Olivia stood up and held onto the table for support. 'You obviously have no idea what kind of a man he is, Uncle Garth. But let me tell you. He mentioned not one *word* of this to me and he spent three days getting an excellent look at the place under completely false pretences!'

'Not if he lost his memory,' Garth replied reasonably, 'but I swore him to silence until I'd had a chance to discuss it with you myself.'

'I don't believe this,' she said faintly, then added with more spirit, 'Believe me, he only lost his memory very selectively!'

'What's that mean?'

'He...' she paused '...he would have known after the first day the significance of Wattle Creek. So that's why he told me things could change and all the rest! *Oh.*' She sat down and ground her teeth.

Garth Lockhart shrugged. 'Even if he did, he kept his word.'

'Well, I'm not going! Uncle Garth,' she cried, 'I know how much this place means to *you*, let alone me. There must be another way.'

'Don't you think I've done all my homework and all the sums, Livvie?' he said painfully. 'Anyway, you're too wrapped up in Wattle Creek, girl,' he added with an attempt to sound bracing. 'Do you the world of good to have a change!'

Olivia stared at him wordlessly and despite his heart problems, despite the fact that she knew he was saying what he had to say, he'd said it too often to her before not to make her blindingly angry with him for an instant.

Then she forced herself to change gear. 'I...I can't think straight.'

'I knew it was going to come as an awful shock to you but I didn't count on you meeting the man and taking a dislike to him,' Garth Lockhart said helplessly.

Olivia breathed deeply.

'But you've got your painting; remember that. And if you still want to be lumbered with an old crock like me we could find somewhere smaller. The thing is, Livvie, at least this way we've got something to sell. You know how many have had to walk off because they hung on too long.'

'Yes,' she murmured, and sat in silent thought. 'On the other hand, we would still have your expertise—'

'We don't know that.'

'Yes, we will,' she said fiercely. 'Don't even think along those lines! What is to stop me running the place with your advice?'

Garth Lockhart sat back tiredly then looked at her with sudden acuteness. 'You're worn out as it is, Livvie, and it's only been a couple of weeks.'

'That's not—' She stopped and bit her lip. And she forced herself to put the ghastly thought of losing Wattle Creek out of her mind for the time being. 'Are you on any medication, Uncle Garth? Has the operation been arranged? That's the most important thing at the moment.'

'In three days' time, I'm afraid, Livvie. They insisted I didn't put it off any longer. And I've got these pills to keep me going in the meantime. I'm supposed not to excite myself either or indulge in alcohol because of the pills, or—' he shrugged '—do anything much at all.'

She rose. 'I'm *sorry* but it…' She shook her head.

'It's not your fault, Livvie. I should have told you sooner; I just didn't know how.'

'Well, I think you should go to bed now, speaking as one who has been told she's a wonderful nurse, and don't worry about me,' she warned gently. 'I'm as tough as old boots, really. Come.'

'There's one more thing, Livvie,' he said tentatively, and she was shaken again at the difference in him.

She raised her eyes heavenwards quizzically in an attempt to amuse him.

'He's coming tomorrow.'

'Ben?'

Garth nodded.

She swallowed.

'You won't antagonize him?'

'Good heavens, no. Now, off to bed with you.'

She paced up and down her studio once she was assured her uncle was asleep. But it was hard to coordinate her thoughts and she found, strangely, that her uppermost feeling was one of helpless incredulity and anger that they could treat her like this.

Men, she thought bitterly. I might as well be a child, let alone a woman! How dare they? I've put as much blood, sweat and tears into this place as anyone...well, relatively—I am only twenty-five but I was mustering when I was twelve!

She sat down on a stool at last and tried to think coherently about Ben Bradshaw. But Caitlin Foster kept getting in the way. And why shouldn't she? she asked herself. We're about the same age, I imagine, but I'm sure she would make a much more glamorous and fitting wife for an international polo star, let alone millionaire. As, I'm also sure, he'll work out in due course. I don't even like polo and all the social bit that goes with it.

As she examined this thought, it brought a strangely sad little smile to her lips. As if it makes the slightest difference to how I really feel about him, she mused. Well, there's also this dreadful, deep pool of anger not only on account of Caitlin Foster but because he's going to be instrumental in turning me off Wattle Creek.

She stared at nothing for a long time, then straightened her spine and took a deep breath. We'll see about that, Mr Bradshaw.

CHAPTER SIX

SHE dressed with care the next morning after making breakfast and doing the chores.

She chose a beige hopsack-linen button-through dress with no sleeves and a collar. The slim lines of the straight dress complemented her figure and she put on a chunky red and black bangle and black patent leather shoes with little red heels.

Her uncle looked relieved when she reappeared not only dressed more formally than usual but with her hair groomed and tidy, and discreetly made up.

Eleven o'clock was the appointed hour, he'd told her, and Ben Bradshaw would be bringing an accountant with him. So she set out a silver tea tray with fine porcelain china and an iced fruit cake.

On the dot of eleven, not Steve Williams this time but Ben himself landed the Pascoe Lyall helicopter beyond the front gate. But Olivia was watching her uncle's expression and she said gently to him, 'Don't overdo things.'

He pressed her hand. 'I won't.'

Then Ben was standing in front of her and she looked up into his eyes and wondered how she could have forgotten how blue they were. 'We meet again, Ben Bradshaw,' she murmured, and put out her hand politely. 'I see your stitches have come out.'

He shook her hand. 'Yes. Good to see you, Olivia,'

he said, and turned to her uncle. 'I don't know if she's told you, sir, but your niece was extremely good to me under very difficult circumstances.'

'It was no more than I'd have done for anybody,' Olivia said with a faint smile, and turned to the other man warmly. 'But come in, please. Tea—' she stopped for a moment frustratedly '—or milk—is ready.'

Garth Lockhart looked at her bemusedly. 'What are you talking about, Livvie? When do we offer our guests milk?'

'I'm afraid I don't drink tea or coffee—Olivia has just remembered, I imagine,' Ben said humorously.

'Then you'll have a beer, man, surely! Why don't we all for that matter?'

'Because you're not supposed to be drinking at the moment, Uncle Garth,' Olivia said serenely, 'so we won't tempt you. Ben can have juice.'

'That's fine with me,' Ben said a shade ruefully but added immediately, 'By the way, this is Mark Bennett, our accountant, and he just happened to mention that he was dying for a cuppa.'

They sat in the lounge while Olivia served the tea and brought Ben a long glass of apple cider. Conversation was general then more pointed on the subject of Garth Lockhart's health. Finally, Ben suggested to Garth that Mark might like to have a look through the books so they went away to Garth's office, leaving Olivia alone to clear up.

But ten minutes later Ben appeared in the kitchen. She glanced across at him standing tall and silent in the doorway, then chose a tin and put the cake into it.

'So, you know the worst of me now, Olivia,' he said quietly, and walked up to the table.

'I hope so,' she murmured. 'Three shocks all on the subject of Ben Bradshaw are enough for anyone, wouldn't you say?'

He stared at her bent head as she put the lid on the tin carefully.

'How long have you known about Wattle?'

'Since last night. He only told me his health was precarious then too. But I don't know why I should have expected any different. I'm obviously just a lay figure in all this. A woman, to make matters worse.'

'He asked me, when he first came to see me, Olivia, to do all in my power not to let any of this leak until he'd had a chance to tell you himself.'

She looked up at last and her grey eyes were scornful. 'So he said. If you imagine that lets you off the hook, I don't.'

He raised a wry eyebrow. 'What would you have done in my position, Olivia?'

'A number of things,' she said after a moment's thought. 'As soon as you remembered—and don't tell me that wasn't pretty early on because I myself happen to have the clearest recollection of what you said about how things can *change*—I would, if I were you, have got myself airlifted off this place immediately and don't tell me you couldn't have arranged that. I would *not* have taken the opportunity to have a good look around under false pretences.'

'Go on,' he invited. 'I feel sure there's more.'

'There is, since you mention it.' She folded her arms and stared at him coldly. 'I certainly wouldn't have sought to *sweeten* someone who you knew very well was going to be devastated, the way you did.'

'"Sweeten",' he said reflectively. 'Is that what you think I was doing?'

'Definitely. What else should I think? Or are you going to tell me Caitlin Foster is a figment of my imagination?'

'But surely I'd have known that would do anything but "sweeten" you, once you found out?'

'Well, it makes no difference anyway,' she said shortly. 'I'm not going without a fight.'

'I don't see how you can, Olivia—'

'I am a shareholder, Ben. You may be able to buy my uncle out but I could be an entirely different matter.'

'You are,' he said with a faint smile. 'And looking very smart this morning, incidentally.'

'Don't patronize me,' she warned. 'Your credibility so far as I'm concerned is in tatters.'

'I can only repeat—I didn't plan *any* of this.'

'There's nothing to be said about the rest of it, but handing Wattle over to you is something I'm not going to take lying down.'

He paused and eyed her narrowly. 'Do you think that's wise, Olivia? Your uncle—'

'I know what you're going to say. Both you and he think you've got me hostage because of his health. But I spoke to his specialist this morning, and he believes there's every chance he'll pull through this operation. Once he feels more like his old self, it could be a different story.'

Ben said nothing but pushed his hands into the pockets of the brown twill trousers he wore with a plain white shirt.

Olivia put the cups in the sink and ignored him.

'I got the sketch framed,' he said presently.

She glanced over her shoulder and shrugged.

'Olivia, I *know* what a shock this must have been and on top of that you're probably feeling foolish about—saying the things you did, to me of all people. But that doesn't mean we can't at least have a civilized discussion.'

'Am I being uncivilized?' she murmured. 'I thought I was being quite calm and collected.'

'But literally simmering just below the surface,' he said dryly. 'Would you sit down and let me explain how unviable Wattle Creek has become?'

'No, I wouldn't!' she said through her teeth, glaring at him. 'Because I not only disapprove of all you represent commercially, I happen to be allergic to polo-playing, pin-up types—but most of all I'm allergic to liars!'

'There are two separate issues there and I'm not a polo-pinup,' he responded evenly. 'Who told you that?'

'It doesn't matter.'

'Yes, it does,' he disagreed. 'I only ever played the game as a hobby and I gave it away years ago. It was never the social side of things that appealed to me, if that's what you're objecting to, but the skills and the horsemanship.'

'You could be a ten handicapper for all I care.'

'But you were the one who brought it up, with palpable disgust,' he said coolly. 'As for the issue of why we kissed each other almost to the point of no return a few days ago—why did you, Olivia?'

'I didn't know about your fiancée at the time, remember?' she said satirically.

'And did you fancy yourself a little in love with me, Livvie Lockhart?'

'Talking of being in love,' she responded swiftly, 'I thought you were a bit in love with yourself and needed taking down a peg or two, Ben.'

'All right,' he said, and it gave her some satisfaction to see the flash of anger that came and went in his eyes. 'Put your proposition, Olivia.'

'What do you mean?'

'Well, your uncle is offering to sell me Wattle Creek—which is one entity under one title. Your shareholding—thirty per cent, I believe—is not in the actual property but in the family company that was formed to operate the station. And as such is not sufficient to block the sale.'

Why the hell didn't I think of that? Olivia asked herself bitterly. Because it never crossed my mind until last night that this could arise.

'Then my proposition is this: the least you owe me, Ben Bradshaw, is the courtesy of waiting until after the operation before you accept the offer.'

'No problem,' he said obligingly. 'I'd already decided to do so in so far as the signing of any contracts goes. But I've given your uncle an assurance that if he's of the same mind once he's up and around I will be of the same mind.'

Olivia took a sudden breath and felt the first glimmer of hope since she'd heard the news the night before.

It was as if he could see it in her eyes, though, because he said, almost gently, 'Things won't change, however.'

'We'll see.' She looked around the kitchen and fiercely willed herself not to give way to the tears that were threatening.

'There is a less painful way we could do this, Olivia.'

'Oh?' Her grey gaze jerked to his.

'I'd be perfectly happy for you and your uncle to stay on in the house. Naturally I'd have to install a manager but he could have his own cottage and there'd be no question of throwing you out before you'd made the necessary adjustments.'

'I think,' she said huskily and looked at him with unmistakable dislike, 'I might hate that more than anything.'

He returned her look dryly. 'You'd see yourself as in the position of being beholden to me—kind of thing?'

'You got it in one, Ben. But that is something I will never be.'

'On the other hand, I think I'd quite enjoy it,' he mused.

She picked up the cake tin with every intention of hurling it at him but sanity prevailed as he simply stared at her, his blue eyes and expression laden with sheer irony.

But the effort to be sane and rational told and she had to turn away to hide the tears of utter frustration that refused to be denied.

He came to stand beside her and, without a word, offered her his handkerchief.

She started to say something scathing then, with a groan, took it and wiped her eyes and blew her nose vigorously. 'I don't usually cry,' she said bitterly, 'but it was quite a shock.' Her shoulders slumped.

'I believe you. It would probably have come as more of a shock if it had come from me.'

'I wonder. Anyway, I wish you'd just go back to your fiancée,' she said bitterly. She balled his hanky up tightly.

'You know, *I* think,' he said conversationally, 'you should take the time to ponder why the thought of my fiancée incenses you so much, Olivia.'

She started to say something and saw the trap—all of which left her gasping for air like a stranded fish.

'Yes,' he agreed gravely. 'So I'll leave you to work on that little conundrum. In the meantime, I believe the operation is to be at John Flynn on the Gold Coast?'

Olivia closed her mouth and swallowed several times. 'Yes,' she said at last. 'It was a question of where to get him in at such short notice and the special facilities they require for it, and the specialist he's been seeing is based there.' She paused and frowned. 'I would have preferred Rockhampton Base Hospital; I've got friends in Rocky and it's much closer but—'

she shrugged helplessly '—the most important thing is what's best for *him.*'

'It's not a problem,' Ben said quietly. 'I've offered to fly him down—saves you driving to Rockhampton or Longreach and getting a commercial flight—and it so happens I have a house at Mermaid Beach. I don't know if you know the Coast that well, but Mermaid Beach isn't far from Tugun and John Flynn.'

'Oh, I couldn't,' Olivia said with real distress and agitation. 'I mean, thank you very much but—'

'Yes, you could,' he said casually. 'Your uncle thinks it's a great idea and it's the *least* I can do after all you did for me. You can have the house to yourself if you so desire.'

Garth Lockhart chose that moment to walk into the kitchen and it was obvious to his niece that he was a much relieved-looking man as he said, 'There you are, you two! Livvie, Ben has very kindly—'

'So he's just told me, Uncle Garth,' she said, desperately trying to inject some enthusiasm into her voice. 'I'm...I'm very grateful.'

A day later Steve Williams flew them to Coolangatta, on the southern end of the Gold Coast, where there was a company car at their disposal. And Garth Lockhart was admitted to the John Flynn hospital, named with some significance in his case, after Flynn of the Inland who had established the Inland Mission and the Royal Flying Doctor Service.

Olivia stayed with him for several hours then he

told her to go home and get some rest. The operation was scheduled for the next morning.

'I'll be back before you go under,' she promised, and kissed him.

It so happened she did know the Gold Coast, having spent many holidays on it during her university career, so it was no problem to drive to Mermaid Beach from Tugun. Steve had presented her with a key to the house although she'd seriously considered booking herself into a motel, but that would have involved giving the hospital a different contact number and possibly alerting her uncle to her state of mind.

Something that was not improved—her state of mind—on discovering that Ben Bradshaw's address was in millionaire's row at Mermaid Beach—a short stretch of absolute beachfront properties that formed some of the dearest real estate on the Coast.

She breathed exasperatedly as she turned the key in the front door. It was a two-storeyed pale grey stucco house and, as she'd known it would be from the address, the vista that greeted her from the front door was magnificent.

Champagne-coloured marble floors flowed towards huge plate-glass windows and a terrace with the beach and ocean beyond. There were ivory wooden louvres folded back at the windows, sumptuous peach couches, elegant mirrors, dark green lacquered walls and occasional tables and exquisite Persian rugs. The sun was setting behind the house and the sea was a calm, placid blue tinged with pink, and fringed with lazy white breakers.

Olivia dropped her single bag and walked to the windows, bitterly regretting that she hadn't packed a swimsuit because she could think of nothing that would have benefited her more than a surf in the sea.

Then she turned and stared around again and tried to imagine Ben Bradshaw in this environment. But what came to mind with astonishing ease was Caitlin Foster. It seemed like a natural setting for her glamour and vibrant beauty.

She bit her lip and willed herself to think along different lines. But no inspiration presented itself and she decided that she couldn't get out of spending a few nights in this mansion but that didn't mean to say she had to be impressed.

Steve had told her that there was a guest bedroom on the ground floor and she went to find it. He'd also told her that a cleaning lady came in daily and replenished the food supply in the house as and when guests were expected, and that she should please feel free to use anything she fancied. He also explained that she'd find a diagram of the security system in the kitchen.

The ground-floor guest bedroom was done out in shades of blue from chalk through to midnight and, she was pleased to discover, had not only an *en suite* bathroom but its own veranda and its own small lounge suite set in front of a concealed television set. I'll camp out here, she thought, and grimaced ruefully, because camping was not an accurate term for it. But she wouldn't have to use the rest of the house apart from the kitchen.

She made herself scrambled eggs for dinner and slept deeply and dreamlessly in the vast blue bed.

It was a long, tiring day the next day but by four o'clock in the afternoon they were able to tell her that her uncle had come through the operation well although he was in Intensive Care and they expected him to have a peaceful night.

She spoke to the specialist and he gave her the news that it would be a couple of days before they could say how successful it had been but he was cautiously optimistic. And he recommended that she go home and get a good night's rest. She also spoke briefly to her uncle but he was sedated and she wasn't sure whether he knew who she was.

So she drove back up the Pacific Highway towards Mermaid Beach at the end of another magnificent day, weather-wise, and, on a sudden impulse, stopped and bought herself a swimsuit.

The house was silent and empty and she donned her purchase, a clear yellow Lycra one-piece suit, and went for a swim.

The surf was wonderfully refreshing and invigorating and she spent about an hour in the water, catching wave after wave or just floating on her back beyond the line of breakers.

It was almost dark when she walked up the beach to where she'd left her towel, shaking and squeezing the moisture out of her hair and unaware that the man sitting patiently beside it was Ben Bradshaw until he picked it up and handed it to her.

She gasped. 'You... I mean... How long have you been here?'

'About twenty minutes.' He rose. 'Enjoy your swim?'

'I...it was marvellous,' she said disjointedly, and wound the towel around her and tucked it in above her breasts. 'But what are you doing here?'

His lips twisted. 'Come to take you out to dinner, Olivia,' he said mildly. 'That's all.'

'But you don't have to and I might not want to go,' she objected. 'In fact I ought not to go anywhere in case the hospital needs to contact me.'

He didn't answer immediately but studied her thoughtfully. They were separated by about a foot of golden sand. He was wearing jeans and a navy blue T-shirt with a white collar. She, on the other hand, was made extremely conscious beneath his slightly narrowed blue gaze of the bare expanse of her legs beneath the towel, of her wet, satiny shoulders and throat, her hair plastered to her head and sending droplets of water down her face.

But, most of all, she was achingly conscious of him and her cheeks started to burn.

'Wet again,' he said idly, and traced the path of a drop of water down her neck with one finger. 'But it has all been arranged,' he added.

She moved out of the reach of that lazy finger. 'What's been arranged?'

'I've spoken to the hospital and given them my mobile phone number in case of an emergency. I believe the news is cautiously optimistic, though?'

'Yes, but they won't know properly for a few days.'

'All the more reason for you to get some R and R, Olivia. Where would you like to go?'

'Ben—this is not necessary.' She bit her lip because it had come out sounding lame.

'On account of me being affianced, a buyer for Wattle or just an all-round cad?' he asked with soft satire.

'Since you mention it, yes,' she replied with more spirit.

He laughed quietly. 'On the other hand, that doesn't mean we couldn't have dinner in some amity. I was always all those things when I helped you put a tarpaulin on the roof, dig a calf out of the mire et cetera but we still managed to have some companionable meals together.'

'Very clever,' she retorted, 'but the difference is I didn't *know* you were all those things at the time.'

'You had the gravest doubts, however. Olivia...' he paused '...do you remember singing me to sleep one night?'

'I...well, yes but...'

'Then I think you should allow me to repay some of that devotion—to duty,' he added with a wicked little glint. 'As a nurse and a hostess, I mean. You can't be feeling a bundle of joy at the moment. In fact, I'm pretty sure you're still shell-shocked, tired and overwound and it would do you the world of good to come out for a quiet meal.'

'And I'm pretty sure you kissed the blarney stone either in this life or a former, Benedict Arnold.' She stopped frustratedly, on the point of telling him he was the last person who could ease her tensions, both personal and otherwise.

He waited for a moment then said placidly, 'Let's go, then.'

'Can I at least get changed?'

'Of course.' He possessed himself of her hand and started to stroll towards the house. 'What do you think of it?'

'Very impressive, what I've seen of it,' she said after a moment, and added with a frown, 'Is this a new strategy?'

'What do you mean?'

'This—chumminess.'

He grinned down at her as they mounted the veranda steps but only said enigmatically, 'Perhaps.'

She hesitated and looked down at his hand around hers.

'Go and change, Livvie Lockhart. Believe me, you'll feel better for a meal.' He released her hand.

She closed herself into the blue bedroom and took a shower. There was a hairdryer attached to the wall and she took her time about drying her hair to her satisfaction then went to survey the few clothes she'd brought with her but there was only one outfit that would do. A pair of slim white trousers and a ribbed, sleeveless, silky-knit top in a dusky pink.

She put on a pair of white flatties and stared at her reflection. Her hair was up as usual and she'd painted her lips barely pink. She brushed aside her fringe with her fingers, and persuaded herself to leave the sanctuary of the blue bedroom.

The main lounge was ablaze with lights, the louvres had been pulled across but tilted open at an angle so bands of dark blue night were visible through them, yet only a distorted view would be available from the beach.

There was a bottle of champagne in a silver cooler on one of the green lacquered coffee tables and Ben was lounging on a settee.

He rose as soon as she appeared and indicated the champagne with a hand.

'I... Why not?' she said a little helplessly, because she was suddenly conscious of feeling powerless. As if everything had drifted out of her control, not least the direction of this evening.

He poured two glasses and brought hers over to the peach couch she'd sunk down upon.

'Thank you,' she murmured as their fingers brushed, but he moved away immediately and sat down opposite.

'Drink it,' he said quietly. 'It'll help.'

She drank half a glass then said with a grimace, 'How did you know? That I needed help.'

He raised an eyebrow. 'Neither Florence Nightingale nor any model of a major-general was anywhere in sight.'

'I must be slipping,' she said ruefully.

'Well, you're not on your home turf either. That could account for it,' he suggested gravely.

She opened her mouth to say that, far from being on her home turf, she was also on Caitlin's turf, but remembered the pledge she'd made never to mention that name to him again.

'What?' he asked.

He had his head propped on a hand and his arm propped on the arm of the couch. His long fingers were playing with his hair and on his temple the marks of the stitches were still visible.

'This is not the kind of setting I had you figured for, somehow, Ben,' she lied, and flinched inwardly because that was as good as mentioning Caitlin's name anyway, she was sure.

But he surprised her. He looked around wryly. 'You're right. Peach couches and acres of marble are not what I'd have chosen myself. My mother is the culprit.'

Olivia's eyes widened in surprise.

'She's convinced there's a Gold Coast style, and this is it.'

'So this is her house?'

'More or less,' he agreed. 'I use it when I need it but she lives here.'

'She doesn't seem to be living here at the moment,' Olivia commented.

He smiled faintly. 'Were you hoping for another chaperon? She's still overseas as it happens. But despite all this opulence you'd like her.'

'Why? I mean, it doesn't matter one way or the other but...' She shrugged.

'You're interested in spite of yourself? I quite understand,' he said with that wicked glint again. 'Uh—she's a very strong-minded lady. She also suffers from vigorous good health although she's in her middle sixties, and when I bought the house for her she informed me that she'd lived in enough farmhouses and station homesteads to be sick of them and she was going to go in the absolute opposite direction with this one.'

Olivia smiled as she looked around again with more interest.

'Did you explore upstairs?' he asked.

'No. I decided to camp out in the blue—' She stopped and added as he looked at her wryly, 'Well, I'm more than ever glad I didn't now. I would have felt as if I was trespassing.'

'Oh, she wouldn't have minded. She's used to guests, I often put people up here for a variety of reasons, business mostly, though, and she enjoys playing hostess. Keeps her young, she says.'

Olivia drank some more champagne. 'You're lucky.'

'I know. Feeling better?'

'Yes. Thanks, but if you're serious about taking me to dinner you'd better do it soon otherwise I'll fall asleep. That's how relaxed I'm feeling at the moment, at least.'

He laughed and stood up. 'We'll walk. That should do the trick.'

So they walked up the pathway beside the beach to Broadbeach, and chose an intimate restaurant that was, he said, renowned for its pasta.

'Of course you make such a mean spaghetti Bolognese yourself, you could be a better judge than most,' he said as they sat down at a table with a red and white checked cloth and a stubby white candle. 'Mean in both senses of the word—you nearly threw it all over me.'

'It was the cream I nearly threw over you,' she said involuntarily.

'Ah—you're right. All the same, that's twice you've been tempted to throw things at me or over me.'

She opened her mouth to reply but the waiter intervened. They made their choices and he ordered a bottle of red wine.

'Did you know that a glass or two of this stuff is supposed to be good for you?' he asked, eyeing her over the rim of his glass.

'So I've read.'

'And did you know that bottling everything up is *not* supposed to be good for you, Olivia?'

She sat back and let her arms hang at her sides for a long moment. Then she said, 'There is one problem; you're the last person who could help. You are, not to put too fine a point on it, the architect of the worst of my problems.'

'I have to disagree but may I, unemotionally, tell you why?'

'Well, I'm not emotional at the moment,' she said shortly, and sipped her wine.

'Not on the surface, perhaps. However...' He paused and looked thoughtful. 'As primary producers, we are about to enter yet another era of difficulty, Olivia. Asian economies are taking a battering at the moment so our exports—live cattle, beef et cetera—are liable to take a battering for a time.'

'Yes.'

'Well, any downturn in the market at this moment, as well as any cause of loss of production, be it drought, flood or whatever, would see Wattle go into the red. And a prolonged downturn would make it impossible for it to survive as is. This is something your uncle has calculated and acknowledged.

'Capital that Wattle doesn't have at the moment is needed for more dams and bores, an injection of new strains of breeding stock and so on. It's also something he's been—trying to hide from you for a while.'

'So I gather,' she said tonelessly.

He watched her narrowly for a moment. 'There are other—forces, if you like, at work, Olivia. His health is obviously one of them but the lack of a family, other than you, is a major player, you could say.'

She sipped her wine and stared unseeingly out over the ocean. 'No heirs,' she murmured with irony, and cast him a swift, enigmatic glance.

'No heirs,' he agreed.

She pushed her fringe aside. 'I don't know what I was supposed to be—an heir factory?'

He looked at her with sudden compassion. 'No, never. And it's not so much your heirs he's regretting—they would have been too young anyway—but the lack of his own. Strong sons. Who knows? They may not have eventuated—but I think it's probably quite a common reaction to regret what may have been.'

'The other thing,' he went on when she made no response, '*is* you. He feels he owes you more than a constant battle from now on to make ends meet. And he also feels a responsibility to the people who work on the station, some of whom you would have to make redundant in the near future whereas I would be able to guarantee them their jobs.'

Olivia flinched.

'I'm sorry,' he said abruptly. 'You may also think I've chosen a bad time to say this but it could be better than for you to go on—'

'Dreaming futile dreams,' she finished for him, and thought for a bit. 'Are you getting a bargain, Ben?'

His mouth hardened. 'Not as much as I might get if you decided to hang on, Olivia.'

'I've made you angry,' she said dryly, 'but I am interested. You must have enormous resources if *you* could carry Wattle through what lies ahead.'

Their meal came at this point. Fettucine marinara for her and ravioli for him. There was a Greek salad with feta cheese and plump black olives, and herb bread. The waiter departed with many flourishes and good wishes for a healthy appetite.

Olivia picked up her fork but only curled the fettucine around it absently.

'I've hedged my bets over the years,' he said presently.

'Where does the Pascoe Lyall come in?' she asked, apropos of nothing.

'Pascoe was my mother's maiden name and Lyall was my father's first name. Eat something, Olivia.'

'I seem to have lost my appetite,' she murmured.

'No, you haven't. It's just a question of making a start and it'll do you good.'

She glinted him a less than friendly little look. 'You seem to have appointed yourself the arbiter of what I should and should not do these days, Ben.'

He raised an eyebrow at her. 'Funny you should say that because I know one thing that would do you the world of good.'

'Really? What might that be?'

'Put it like this,' he said slowly, and stared at the salad for a long moment. Then he raised his eyes to hers and they were, to her surprise, quite serious. 'After we've eaten, a walk back along the beach would be beneficial. Then if you'd like a nightcap we could have one on the terrace whilst we watched the moon—did you know it was full moon tonight?'

'No.'

'It is.' He smiled faintly. 'And then, since you've adopted the blue bedroom, we could retire to it and I could run my hands up and down your body as I did once before, and take your clothes off slowly. And we could do the thing we've been dying to do—we could make love with all the passion I know you're capable of and we could blend it with the things that make us laugh together—you could even sing to me again, Olivia.'

A tremor ran through her body that she was unable to conceal.

He said nothing but his eyes told her he hadn't missed it.

'You don't—' She moistened her lips and started again. 'You don't feel that's above and beyond the call of duty, Ben? For you, I mean?'

'I can assure you duty has nothing to do with it, Olivia.'

'It must,' she protested. 'Otherwise, how would you describe yourself, Ben? I can't quite think of it at the moment but there has to be a name for a man who is unfaithful to a woman even *before* the wedding.'

'Some would say better before than after, but...' he paused and toyed with his glass '...I'm not one of them. Therefore, there is to be no wedding. Caitlin and I have broken our engagement.'

CHAPTER SEVEN

'MADAM is not enjoying the marinara? If it is not to her liking I will replace it with *anything* of her choice,' the waiter said effusively as Olivia stared open-mouthed at Ben. 'You have only to say the word. A guest of Mr Bradshaw is our first priority.'

She closed her mouth then said hastily, 'No, thank you, it's fine.' She started to eat.

'Well, we've achieved something,' Ben remarked as the waiter left, reassured.

'I'm speechless,' Olivia responded, and continued to eat.

'I would have thought I'd earned your approval.'

'How can you say that? How...could you just do it like that? Is she...?' She stopped.

'Is she...?' he prompted.

Olivia put her fork down and drank some wine. 'Devastated, for example?' Her gaze was sardonic.

'Not really,' he replied, and finished his ravioli.

'Oh, I see. Only partially?'

He reached for his glass and stared at it absently. 'That could be the purpose of an engagement. To find out how well suited you really are, before you tie the knot.'

'I'm afraid I've thought of it a little differently—and not so long ago you could have got yourself sued for breach of promise, Ben.'

147

He smiled slightly.

'How can you sit there and be so calm about it?'

He raised a wry eyebrow. 'I didn't say I was calm about it.'

'But you must have loved her—why ask her to marry you otherwise? And then to break it off all because of a bump on the head! That's insane.'

'Not so insane,' he said slowly. 'But if you've had enough I feel there might be better places to have this discussion—especially if you're going to get even more hot and bothered about it.'

She breathed raggedly then looked around to see a few curious gazes directed their way. 'Let's go,' she said through her teeth. 'But I am not going to go to bed with you, Benedict Bradshaw, if for no other reason than because you appear to me to be a womanizer of the highest order.'

'Womanizer,' he mused quizzically. 'That could be the word you were looking for earlier.'

She got up and walked out.

He caught her up five minutes later as she strode along the pathway, oblivious to the delights of a full moon and its golden pathway across the sea.

'You've broken Angelo's heart, Olivia.' He stepped into place at her side.

'Blow Angelo,' she said. 'What about Caitlin's heart?'

'Essentially, that's between me and Caiti, but I don't believe I have broken her heart.'

Olivia refused to look at him and kept striding out.

He loped along beside her then stopped suddenly. 'This is it.'

Olivia looked up at the house. 'I don't want to go in.'

'That's childish, Olivia.'

'No it's not. I just—I don't know what to think.' She closed her eyes and shook her head dazedly.

He held up the long packet she hadn't noticed he was carrying. 'Angelo insisted we take the wine, since we'd had barely a glass each. Let's sit on the terrace and discuss this. You can always run away down the beach if things get too much for you.'

'Don't kid yourself that I wouldn't, Ben,' she warned.

He brought two glasses and poured the wine.

It was a still, warm night and the surf was rhythmic and soothing. As they sat in silence they saw the twinkling lights of a plane flying low and parallel to the coast on its final approach to Coolangatta Airport.

It made Olivia think of her uncle because Coolangatta was next door to Tugun.

Ben must have read her thoughts because he put his mobile phone on the table. 'Would you like to ring the hospital? I've put the number into the memory bank.'

She nodded gratefully and he got the hospital for her.

She handed the phone back to him a couple of minutes later. 'He's resting comfortably.'

'Good.' He pushed the aerial down and closed it. 'Olivia, about Caiti.'

'I thought it was between you and her.'

'I'm not planning to burden you with the intimate details but, yes, I did think I—should marry her. I never spoke a truer word, however, when I told *you* that I wasn't sure how being in love survived being married. Do you remember?'

'I…yes. It was something we agreed upon.'

'So we did. And for a variety of reasons that bump on the head and what happened whilst I had no recollection of her made me see that we wouldn't last the distance, Caiti and I.'

'Why?' Olivia asked intensely. 'You couldn't remember anything for a time, so you said, not even your name. That doesn't mean…anything!'

He cast her a quizzical little glance then put his hands behind his head and stretched his legs out. 'Perhaps not. But, for whatever reason, I found myself wondering why we kept postponing our marriage.'

Olivia moved suddenly and looked at him narrowly. 'She said… I mean…' She trailed off.

'She said something like that to you?'

'Well, yes, but—' She stopped and shrugged. 'I didn't believe it meant anything.'

'What it meant was this—we were both afraid of taking that final step. Caiti because of what she would have to give up and me because—whilst she's lovely and amusing, stunning to squire around and perhaps the kind of glamorous girl I thought I ought to be marrying, and we were good in bed—I was conscious of a lack.'

Olivia reached a little blindly for her glass. 'Poor Caiti,' she murmured.

'Only I couldn't find a name for it,' he said sombrely. 'And it wasn't a lack in her so much as in me. Because I'd tried to bury a certain cynicism on the subject of love and marriage, I'd pretended to myself that we had enough going for each other to have a marriage that was probably as good as it was going to get.'

'That is cynical,' Olivia said involuntarily.

He looked at her briefly then shrugged. 'There were other, humorous pressures.'

'Such as?'

'If you've ever felt like a prospective heir factory, my mother, whose only child I am, is positively thirsting for grandchildren. She was convinced that Caiti and I would have lovely offspring.'

Olivia stared at him. 'Well, *she* obviously had no reservations about you marrying Caitlin.'

'No, but that's because she has some quite severe reservations about me in general.' He reached for his glass.

'I don't understand.'

He gazed at the path of moonlight on the water. 'She and my father were very young when they married. Twenty-one and twenty-two; she was the older.'

He paused and grimaced. 'And that's the way she believes it should happen—not that the wife should be older but that when you get to the grand old age of *thirty-three* you're spoilt, capricious, jaded and cynical. She told me to thank my lucky stars Caiti had come along because if I hadn't found the right wife by now I most probably never would—according to what I was mistakenly looking for.'

'And you tended to believe her?'

'Yep,' he said.

'Then all I can say is—it's just as well you got a bump on the head, Ben.' Olivia shook her head and finished her wine.

'That's a change of heart.'

'Not really. I'm more than ever convinced you're a womanizer but I now see that Caitlin has had a lucky escape.'

'Well, we're agreed there.'

'Yes, but does *she*…?'

'She was actually nerving herself to tell me that we couldn't get married for another four months at least, because she'll be filming on location about a thousand miles away and will only be able to be home on the weekends.' He poured the last of the wine.

Olivia blinked.

'Are you speechless again?' he drawled.

'I…this doesn't have anything to do with me…'

He smiled. 'Dear Livvie Lockhart, you have an astonishingly short memory!'

'Why do you only call me Livvie in conjunction with Lockhart?'

'As a *non sequitur* that was almost inspired,' he said with soft satire.

'But why?' she persisted stubbornly, although her cheeks reddened.

'I like Olivia. I think it suits you and I think I shall always call you that unless I'm teasing you or I'm reminded that you're Livvie to everyone else. It will be a good way of keeping those private things between us—very private.'

'Ben,' she said helplessly, 'you don't seriously imagine that the fact that you've cast off your fiancée and admitted what amounts to your *knowing* it wasn't true love anyway recommends you to me?'

He stared at her.

'On top of,' she added precisely and with a lot more feeling, 'the shameful scam you pulled about how much of your memory was actually lost, not to mention every other thing I mistrust and dislike about you.'

There was a long silence. Then he said coolly, 'Would you rather I propositioned you differently?'

'Differently? How?' She frowned at him.

'I could offer to buy a share of Wattle Creek rather than the whole caboodle, on one condition. That you consent to be my mistress.'

She gasped and stood up abruptly. 'I would never, *ever* agree to anything like that!'

'It would solve all your problems in one go, though,' he said lazily. 'Your uncle could live out the rest of his life on a station he loves. You could do the same, surrounded by all the history of the Lockhart family that means so very much to you.' He paused and looked at her with irony. 'And it would take care of whatever it was that prompted you to kiss me so very passionately in the creek— Sit down,' he added with just a hint of menace as she looked longingly at the empty wine bottle.

'You can't order me around—'

'In the interests of my own safety, yes, I can. Don't

forget you've already thought about braining me with a cake tin. But, although I hesitate to point it out—I'm sure it will go down as another black mark against me—I am a lot stronger than you are, Olivia.'

She gasped again, but although he gave no sign of being about to leap up and overpower her she got the distinct feeling that she shouldn't put it past him.

She sank down. 'You're despicable, Ben Bradshaw.'

'I may be; I'm also the man you want, if you would allow yourself to be honest.' He shrugged. 'As I want you.'

'Want,' she said scathingly. 'Don't you think you got yourself into enough trouble the last time you tried to convince yourself that was enough?'

He chuckled suddenly but she was not to know what he was going to say because his phone rang.

It was the hospital to say that her uncle had had a sudden relapse.

'I'll take you,' he said quietly.

'No, I—'

'Olivia, don't argue.'

She didn't.

It was mid-morning the next day by the time they got back to the house at Mermaid Beach. Garth Lockhart had survived emergency surgery but the fact that they'd had to operate again was not good news.

Ben had insisted on staying with her throughout the long night, and he said, as she stood in the foyer of his mother's house looking white and exhausted, 'Bed for you, my dear. But take this first.'

'What is it?'

'A mild sleeping pill. I asked them for it.'

'Thanks. And thank you for all you've done. But I think I should stay awake in case—'

He smiled slightly and touched her cheek gently. 'I'll do that and I'll wake you if necessary. Off you go.'

The sun was setting as she swam up out of a deep sleep.

She lay still for a while as all the events of the last twenty-four hours filtered through her mind and a question came to her lips—what do you do with a man like Ben Bradshaw?

How to separate the fun side of him or the way he'd sat with her through the long dark hours of the night…getting her coffee, talking when she wanted to talk, about a wide variety of things, pushing two chairs together so she could lie down for a while…from the other side of him?

From the man who suggested you become his mistress in return for being able to stay on Wattle, she reminded herself brutally. Who lied to you by omission.

She got up at last and pulled her yellow costume on, hoping that a swim in the sea might clear her head.

He was reading on the main terrace as she came out of the house. He had his feet propped up on a table and he was wearing a pair of navy board shorts, no shirt and dark glasses.

She hesitated but he must have heard her because

he put his book down and removed the glasses to look around.

'Ah. Feeling better?'

'Yes, thank you. Any news?'

'He's resting comfortably once again—can I come too?'

Olivia sighed with relief then she blinked at him. 'Come?'

'For a swim?'

'Of course. It's going to be another lovely evening.'

'Yep!'

They stepped down onto the sand together and moments later were plunging into the water.

'Almost as good as Wattle Creek!' he called to her over the surf, then set out in a fast crawl to beyond the breakers.

She followed.

'You swim really well for a girl brought up beyond the black stump.'

They paddled in the calm water. 'My boarding-school saw to that.' She dived under the water and came up to flip onto her back. 'They also taught me how to play tennis.'

'Now that—would be interesting.'

'How so?' She moved her arms gently to keep herself afloat.

'I play a mean game of tennis myself.'

'I imagine you would. So, tennis, polo—what else do you do?'

'Oddly enough I've never been any good at golf. It doesn't suit my temperament.'

'Why not?' she asked quizzically.

He swam right up to her and his eyes were as blue as the sea beneath wet, spiky lashes. 'Trying to thrash a tiny white ball about the place for hours frustrates me unbearably.'

'What about polo balls—?

'Pucks, they're not balls.'

'Sorry, pucks, then. And tennis balls?'

'They're bigger and you can have a really good go at them and you can smash them around to relieve your feelings.'

'Are you saying you're too impatient for golf?' she queried with a smile.

'Patience is not a virtue I'm renowned for.'

She laughed, sank and came up spluttering.

'Do you think that's funny?'

'Yes—I don't know why,' she confessed. 'Well, I do; I just had this mental image of you behaving atrociously on a golf course then charming everyone witless.'

He looked injured. 'That's not a very nice thing to say, Olivia.'

'Don't tell me you don't know just how to charm people witless— Don't answer,' she said with a grin. 'I bet I can beat you back to the beach!' And she started to swim furiously.

He turned to see what she had seen behind him— a perfect breaker forming—and with his long, powerful strokes caught it as she did and they surfed marvellously all the way into the beach.

They lay side by side at the tide mark, he on his back, she propped on her elbows as they got their breath back and the water washed gently over them up to their waists.

'Aren't you tired?' she asked.

'I had a couple of hours' sleep—with my phone right beside me.'

'I suppose you're one of those people who don't need a lot of sleep either.'

He turned to look at her with a grimace. 'Is that another black mark?'

'No. I'm just trying to figure you out, Ben Bradshaw.'

'I don't think I'm that difficult to figure out. The difficulty comes from the circumstances in which we met.'

'Could I ask you a favour?'

'Be my guest.'

She hesitated.

He took the opportunity to say, 'Let me guess. No more talk of asking you to be my mistress for the moment?' He turned over, propped his chin on his hands and looked into her eyes. They were only inches apart.

And lying so close to him as the ripples came and went suddenly caused Olivia to be almost overwhelmed by sheer desire.

The skin of his shoulders and arms was sleek and golden, more tanned than she remembered. And the muscles beneath them lay taut and powerful. His back was smooth although his chest was sprinkled with dark hair, his legs long and powerful too.

And she thought that she would like nothing more than to be intensely physical with Ben Bradshaw right there and then. Because her body was developing an ache of sheer longing to be handled and pulled close, to be possessed, and a feeling of lovely anticipation grew and spread through her just at the thought of it.

'Olivia?'

She swallowed and stood up. 'Yes, please. If you wouldn't mind. I don't seem to be able to handle it too well at the moment—' She broke off and bit her lip at the utter irony of what she'd said and sent a swift prayer heavenwards that he wouldn't read her mind.

'On one condition,' he murmured, and stood up himself.

'What's that?' she asked warily.

He looked her over, from her dripping hair down to her toes and all her figure beneath the clinging yellow Lycra in between, but as she went to move awkwardly away he said gravely, although a smile touched his eyes, 'That you'll let me cook you dinner.'

'I…I didn't know you cooked,' she said lamely.

'There's a lot you don't know about me but let's not go into that—as a matter of fact, I don't, well, not that well.'

'But you just offered…*to* cook me dinner.'

'If you would help I'm sure I could manage it. Let me tell you what I had in mind.' He took her hand and started to walk towards the house. 'Prawns, rice and a salad.'

Olivia glanced at him through her lashes. 'Go on— do you have any prawns, or is that another figment of your imagination like your cooking?'

'I popped out while you were fast asleep and purchased three dozen of the finest prawns,' he told her. 'And I'm sure there's rice in the house as well as salad ingredients. I also bought a crusty brown loaf.'

'Green prawns or cooked prawns?' she enquired.

'Green—fresh off a trawler, they told me.'

'I—well, I do—know a good way of doing them.'

'I knew I could rely on you, Livvie Lockhart,' he said with infinite satisfaction.

'Did you, now? I have to tell you you're going to be the one to peel them, however, Ben,' she said seriously. 'Then they should be marinated for a while.'

'I'm yours to command.'

They went straight to the kitchen because, as Olivia suggested, they could shower and change while the prawns were marinating.

'Leave the tails on,' she instructed, 'and butterfly them.'

'How?'

She peeled a prawn and slit it down the back so that it opened out into a butterfly shape. 'That's how.'

'Hmm… OK, but it's going to take me a lot longer than you.'

'Unlike you, I have a lot of patience,' she said serenely. 'And I'm not the one who offered to cook dinner under completely false pretences. Just take your time,' she advised.

'I'm sure you can be a right tyrant, Olivia,' he commented.

She tucked her towel around her more securely and

assembled the ingredients for the marinade in his mother's pale grey, dream kitchen.

'I am good at instructing people now you come to mention it so I'll tell you how to make this. Take a bowl.' She showed him the stainless-steel bowl she'd found. 'Pour in some sesame seed oil, some soy sauce and crush in half a clove of garlic. You could also add some white wine if you were so minded but I won't bother.'

'Why not? We could drink the rest of it.'

'I seem to spend a lot of time drinking with you these days, but it's your wine.' She shrugged.

He got a bottle from the wine rack and opened it for her. 'I'll chill it before we get really decadent and have a glass or two,' he murmured, and went back to the prawns. 'Then what?'

'That's it, for the marinade. I'll do the rice now and the salad.'

'Won't the rice get cold?'

'I find it's actually better to cook rice first, in the microwave, then heat it up just before you serve it. It comes out even nicer and fluffier.'

'I could become a gourmet cook if this keeps up.'

She didn't answer and he eyed her back thoughtfully at the same time as he wondered if she knew how revealing her grey eyes were. How they'd widened when they'd been lying side by side in the water and he could have sworn the same thoughts were running through her mind as were running through his. Still, he cautioned himself, the longer I can keep this kind of friendliness up, the harder it's going to be for you to resist, Livvie Lockhart, did you but know it.

Because, for reasons you may not care to know about, I intend to have you one day, and willingly.

She turned suddenly and their gazes locked. He said nothing and neither did she until she made a curious little gesture, as if to cut the contact that seemed to be flowing between them, and reached for a knife.

'You peel, I'll butterfly them,' she murmured. 'Otherwise we will be here all night.'

Half an hour later the prawns were marinating, the salad was made, the rice done, and Olivia thankfully retreated once more to the blue bedroom.

Not that anything momentous took place, she thought, then corrected herself swiftly. Yes, it did! We looked at each other with no pretence, no dissemination and he knew how I felt just as *I* know there's an electric field around us at times that's devastatingly sensual. How long can I resist it?

But I haven't even had time to think properly about the breaking of his engagement to Caitlin, his diabolical offer to make me his mistress—I'm still unable to believe I'm about to lose Wattle Creek, really believe it, she mused. How could so much happen in the space of a week, roughly?

She threw her towel down, entered the bathroom and peeled off her costume with her mind far from what she was doing. But she finished off her shower with a needle spray of cold water that made her gasp but would, hopefully, restore some sharpness of mind to her.

And the first thing she did when she came out of the shower was ring the hospital. Prawns or no prawns, that was where she should be, she decided. But the excellent staff thought otherwise, it seemed.

'The doctor has just seen him and is much happier with his condition now, Miss Lockhart,' the ward sister told her. 'But we're keeping him sedated and will do throughout the night. There's no point in you spending another night here—get a good rest, my dear.'

'I had a rest today—'

'All the same, conserve your strength while you have the chance, there'll be quite a long convalescence for you to cope with.'

'If you're very sure?' Olivia said.

'I am.'

She put the phone down and stared at it rather helplessly. That was plan A, she reflected. Plan B? Well, the prawns at least, I guess.

'Nice,' Ben said approvingly as she walked into the lounge.

Olivia looked down at herself ruefully. She had on a long, floating dress in a cool mint cotton with cream and pink swirls on it. 'I made it myself,' she murmured.

'Ah. Another plus,' he commented, and handed her a tall glass that was almost as artistically swirled as her dress.

She took it and raised an eyebrow at him.

'A cocktail of my own concocting.'

'Not one that leaps up and bites you when you least expect it, I hope?'

He considered. 'Not really. It's mostly pineapple

juice and cream with a dash of Cointreau and crème de menthe.'

'No wonder it's so pretty.'

'Sit down, Olivia,' he invited. 'You look as if you're poised for flight.'

She glanced at him coolly and sat down on a peach couch with as much composure as she could muster. 'I rang the hospital again.' She told him what the sister had said.

'Well, that's good news—apart from the long convalescence bit.'

'Yes.'

'But he couldn't be better placed with someone like you to look after him.'

Olivia sipped some of the cocktail and found it was delicious. But she put it down on the table in front of her and brushed back her fringe. 'I don't know about that. I feel very guilty about not realizing something was seriously wrong with him. So much for my nursing skills.'

'He told me he'd done his best to hide it from you.'

'I know. I used to rub embrocation on his back and nag at him to do muscle-strengthening exercises.' She shrugged. 'I can't tell you how foolish that makes me feel.'

'I think you're being too hard on yourself, Olivia.'

She glanced up at him. He was lounging on the opposite couch and he'd changed into blue and black checked shorts and a black T-shirt. 'I think, as it happens,' she said slowly, 'that there's another reason for it.'

He looked at her narrowly. 'Such as?'

'What everyone seems to be accusing me of these days.' She picked up her glass and took another sip. 'I was so wrapped up in Wattle Creek and preserving the homestead et cetera, I was blind, figuratively, to just about anything else.'

He said nothing but she didn't miss the sudden look of compassion in his eyes. Which is tantamount to agreeing with me, she told herself, and flinched inwardly. Because the last thing she wanted was his compassion, either.

'So, I'm presented with a real dilemma,' she murmured. 'But the thing is—' she looked at him again '—I still have to pinch myself to believe any of this is real.'

'Have you been able to think about anything I said?' he queried.

'Such as your offer to buy only part of Wattle if I'd consent to be your mistress? Believe me, I need to do a lot more than pinch myself to make that seem real. Could I be right in hoping you said it in the heat of the moment?'

He laughed softly. 'As a matter of fact I was slightly annoyed at the time. Although—' there was a sudden acuteness in his eyes that she didn't miss '—it *would* solve certain things.'

It hit Olivia with almost the same force her brain seizure on the bank of the creek had—only this time it's sanity, not the opposite, she thought bitterly. But there is only one thing to do because I am never again going to put myself through the pain of…waking up to being in love with this man only to be confronted by the evidence of how unattainable he is…

Because even if he has shed his fiancée I can't exactly applaud it, and to think of me only in mistress terms—well, it speaks for itself besides being thoroughly despicable!

'Thank you,' she said quietly, 'but the answer is no. I feel quite sure we wouldn't suit.'

'Even though we can barely keep our hands off each other, Olivia?' he drawled. 'You have some strange notions.'

A flame of anger licked through her. 'Do you think so? You know, I'm reminded of something you said to me—if this isn't a duel for dominance, if this isn't something even worse such as sheer blackmail—I'm a Dutchman, Ben.'

He regarded her thoughtfully for a long moment. 'So what do you have in mind?'

She took a breath. 'The only thing I can do—give in gracefully.' She closed her eyes briefly then forced herself to open them and look directly at him. 'I won't oppose the sale of Wattle.'

He raised his eyebrows. 'That would put us on neutral territory, Olivia,' he said dryly, 'but it's a little surprising in view of what *you* once said to me.'

'I'm not interested in putting us on neutral territory,' she said tautly, and breathed raggedly as she tried to gather her thoughts. 'And what I said to you about being dragged off kicking and screaming— don't imagine I won't be screaming inside but—it's come home to me that I have been remiss and put a place before people and—there's nothing else I can do.'

'So, becoming the lover of a man you want is too high a price to pay even for Wattle Creek?'

'Simply—yes.' She opened her hands and closed them.

'Well, I admire you for that. Drink some more of your cocktail,' he suggested. 'Even if only for medicinal purposes.'

'I might choke— What do you *mean* you admire it? You were the one who suggested it!'

He shrugged and smiled a wry little smile. 'I have the feeling you'd make a very troublesome mistress, Olivia. Yes, I feel one would wonder what one had taken on! But, in point of fact, I don't run to mistresses; I'm not really that kind of man,' he murmured.

Olivia stood up carefully. 'Ben Bradshaw, if you were testing me, if you feel you have the right to test me like that—oh! I could kill you.'

'That's nothing new,' he said with a lurking little smile. 'By the way, having gone to all that trouble, should we now cook our masterpiece?'

But Olivia could only stand transfixed, as pale as paper and with her eyes huge and dark.

He sobered, stood up abruptly and came towards her.

'Don't...' she whispered.

'Don't be a fool,' he said roughly. 'What do you think I'm going to do?'

'I don't know but—'

'Look, sit down before you faint,' he ordered, then simply picked her up and sat her down and sat down beside her. 'Here.' He put the glass in her hand and guided it to her lips.

She hesitated then drank and felt the colour returning to her face.

He said, 'Would you tell me one thing at least, Olivia? It might—' he grimaced '—just rein in the Machiavellian side of my nature.'

She glanced at him suspiciously. 'What?'

'*I* am exceedingly troubled to be sitting next to you, drinking in the perfume of your skin and hair, having the feel of your body on my fingertips, the taste of your lips on mine and a host of other memories but *not* having an admission from you that things could be the same for you.'

She swallowed, moved restlessly but said nothing.

'Let's try another tack, then. What is so difficult about making such an admission?'

It was as if his words had opened up the channels of all her sensory perceptions. Their shoulders were brushing and she could feel the warmth of his body on her skin, she too could breathe the clean male tang of his skin and feel the taste of his lips on hers, the hardness of his body against her own soft slenderness, the crispness of his dark hair in her fingers…

'I…' She paused and turned to look into his eyes to find them serious for once and with his question mirrored in them. 'I…know where it would lead if I made that admission,' she said huskily. 'But for all the wrong reasons.'

'What could be so wrong about it, Olivia?' he said quietly, and, as she went to look away, put a long finger under her chin.

She closed her eyes then lifted her lashes. 'How can you not know, Ben? Only days ago you were engaged to another girl. Only—well, in the near future you'll own Wattle and I'll be gone from it—yes, it might be the sensible thing and all the rest but I'll never be able to disassociate that from you and I can't applaud the way you've broken your engagement.'

'In other words—you could never forgive me, Olivia?' He released her chin.

'No.' She sipped some more of her cocktail. 'I think I know myself well enough to know...that.'

'I see.' He sat back. 'So you're saying there could be no future for us?'

She nodded.

'And that's all I'm going to get,' he murmured wryly. 'Oh, well, you win some and lose some—shall we cook?'

The prawns were delicious.

They ate outside on the terrace and it was curiously companionable. He told her about his interests in Argentina and quite a lot about his life in general.

'Are you based at Charleville?' she asked.

'The Queensland division of the company is—we have a property there and an office—but I spend a lot of time in Brisbane, Sydney and Melbourne.'

'So where do you call home?'

He looked at her meditatively. 'Nowhere, really. I have apartments in a couple of places and this.' He gestured to the house.

'Not even the place you grew up?'

'I grew up in a lot of different places,' he said hu-

morously. 'That's why I'm such a gregarious, eclectic
character.'

'Outback properties, though?'

'Mostly,' he agreed. 'Uncle Garth said you'd
been to all the right schools et cetera.'

He raised a wry eyebrow then grinned wickedly.
'That could account for me being such a polished,
well-spoken, well-presented kind of bloke. As a matter of fact I even have good teeth.'

She had to laugh although something felt as if it
was bleeding to death inside her.

But he seemed to be unaware of her inner turmoil
although she was conscious that he was going out of
his way to smooth the path of the evening for her in
the charming and funny way that only he could.

They tidied up the kitchen together and when it was
done she stood in the middle of it and wondered how
to say goodnight.

He did it for her. 'Bed, I think, Livvie Lockhart.
Goodnight—but one thing before you go.'

She looked at him. They were separated by a couple of feet, and he was leaning back against a counter
with his arms folded across his black T-shirt.

She licked her lips. 'What?'

'There's only one thing for you to worry about at
the moment and that's getting your uncle well again.'

'I...' she brushed back her fringe '...I think I may
have learnt that lesson, Ben.'

He paused and let his blue gaze travel down her
long dress and she felt herself tense inwardly, but all
he said was, 'If you ever need—assistance, all you
have to do is ask, Olivia.'

'Thank you,' she said very quietly, 'but I'll be fine. Goodnight.' She walked away.

But she cried herself to sleep in the blue bedroom because she knew she'd never forget Ben Bradshaw even if he was a womanizer and everything else she held against him. Because there would be so many memories to haunt her—Ben and Bonnie, the creek, this house and their swim, but also those words that would torment her: 'you win some and lose some'.

He was gone when she got up the next morning.

There was a note stuck on the fridge with a fish-shaped magnet that made no excuses or apologies for his departure but said simply that she was to avail herself of the house for as long as was necessary, and gave a number to call when she needed Steve to fly them back to Wattle Creek.

She took it off the fridge and read it through a blur of tears—there was only one personal touch to it. He'd signed himself Benedict Arnold.

She was about to screw it up and throw it in the bin when something held her back and she found herself doing the strangest thing. She raised it to her lips and kissed it gently. But then she straightened her shoulders and tore it up.

So that's that, she thought, and went to ring the hospital.

CHAPTER EIGHT

TEN days later Steve Williams was flying them back to Wattle Creek in a Pascoe Lyall fixed-wing aircraft.

Olivia watched the landscape unfold beneath them. They flew over Emerald, well named with its orchards, vineyards and cotton crops, then over the range to drier country where the colours were subtler and straggling fences and telephone wires went for miles upon miles. And finally the scrub country gave way to the Mitchell grass plains that were home to Wattle Creek Station.

Garth Lockhart, she noticed, was drinking in the landscape as well and she felt her heart contract with pity. But she'd set herself a course and it resolutely refused to encompass bitterness or regret. His doctors had been happy with the outcome of the second operation in the end and had predicted that, if he took things easily, there was a good chance of years ahead for him.

And there was a welcoming committee waiting for them on the airstrip. As Olivia saw them all lined up, she had to breathe deeply to maintain her composure, and to remind herself that at least all these familiar faces would be taken care of.

Three weeks later, the flying doctor paid one of his regular visits to Garth and drew Olivia aside after-

172

wards.

She looked at him anxiously. 'Is there a problem?'

'No, Livvie. I just wanted to tell you you've done a great job. By my reckoning and the tests we've been doing, he's as well as he could be under the circumstances, and provided you can restrain him from leaping about the place he can live a normal life now. In other words you can relax—you look as if you could do with it too,' he added.

She breathed a sigh of relief.

'You'll still need to keep up the diet but it's worth it not only from his heart and arterial point of view, but having lost the weight he has can only do him good.'

'OK.' But as she said it brightly she felt a creeping feeling of dread.

Because, as if by mutual consent, she and her uncle hadn't talked much about the coming move from Wattle during this period of convalescence. They'd idly discussed living on the coast, not the Gold Coast but somewhere round Mackay close to the beautiful Whitsunday Passage, but that was about as far as it had got although she had discreetly started to turn out drawers and cupboards. But with this medical clearance she knew it could no longer be put off.

Something stopped her from taking the plunge, however. A couple more days of this peace and tranquillity can only benefit him, she told herself. And two then three days slid by. Then their weekly mail arrived and he came to find her with a letter in his hand and a stunned expression on his face.

She was in the kitchen lining cake tins. Christmas was only a few weeks away.

'Livvie—Livvie, sit down, girl, will you?'

She looked at him frowningly. 'Why?'

'The most amazing thing,' he said, and sat down himself. 'No, no, let me read it again in case I'm dreaming—if you had a cup of tca handy that might help.'

She shrugged and made the tea. 'OK, before I die of curiosity, spill the beans,' she said lightly and with not the slightest premonition.

Garth Lockhart stared at the letter again then said, 'Livvie, Ben Bradshaw has made us a proposition.'

She stiffened slightly.

'Instead of buying the whole of Wattle, he's offered to buy into the holding company which means in effect that we will still be shareholders but the injection of capital we need will be assured—and we won't have to leave.'

Olivia clenched her hands around her cup and winced as she spilt some tea over them. 'But...I mean, under what conditions, Uncle Garth?'

'None,' he said simply. 'I'll still have a say in the running of the place but I won't have to do any of the work. He's suggested promoting Jack to station manager and bringing him in an assistant to take a lot of the pressure off me—and you.'

For a moment she felt as if she couldn't breathe. Then she made herself say, 'But...how will you feel not having the ultimate say as you've had for so long?'

'I can work with Ben,' he assured her. 'I always

did like the stamp of a man he is. When I first went to see him, before you ever met him, I expected to have to deal with some hard-nosed, entirely profit-orientated businessman but he wasn't like that. He knew what he was talking about when it came to the country and beef production, but not only that, he was courteous and respectful. I was also expecting to be made to feel as if I was going cap in hand but he made me feel quite different.'

Olivia licked her lips. 'How so?'

'Well...' Garth paused reminiscently 'as if all my experience was valuable and of interest to him. I just didn't feel like some broken-down old codger who was about to go broke although I wasn't far from it.'

Is this what it's like to have to eat humble pie? Olivia thought. But how to deal with this? How to handle being often in contact with him again, unless...? No...

'And he's mentioned expressly that the homestead would be considered part of our shareholding. In other words, anything you want to do with it will be up to you.'

'I...can't believe this,' she said barely audibly, but one glance at Garth Lockhart revealed a new man.

And he said softly, 'Oh, Livvie, I've seen you getting around as if your heart was broken although you've tried to put such a brave front on it. I thought I knew how much Wattle meant to you— I didn't know the half of it. But you've got it back, girl!'

If only you knew, Olivia thought, and made herself swallow some tea. Knew that leaving Wattle turned out to be a mild cause of pain compared to losing Ben Bradshaw. And now this.

'When do we have to decide?' she asked.

'What's to decide?' her uncle said gaily. 'But he's coming to see us tomorrow. About lunchtime, he reckons.'

It was a baking hot day the next day, with the sky a pale, shimmering blue.

When Garth was ready to drive down to the airstrip to meet the plane, Olivia told him she still had a few things to do to get lunch ready. He took this unsuspectingly in his stride and was not to know that everything for lunch was perfected and that his niece had nothing to do at all but wait with her nerve-ends screaming.

She heard the plane fly overhead and wandered out of the kitchen because she felt unbearably claustrophobic. And she was standing under a shady gum tree when she saw a vehicle pull up at the front gate of the garden. She frowned because it wasn't the air-conditioned Land Rover her uncle had used but one of the station utilities. Only one person was in it—Ben.

She watched with her heart hammering like a tomtom as he got out, looked around and saw her. And her limbs locked although she would have dearly loved to run away as he clicked the gate open and walked towards her.

Then he was right in front of her, all the lean, tall, vital stuff of her dreams in khaki trousers, boots and a yellow T-shirt but with his blue eyes unusually sombre.

And he took in the cool pink and grey sundress she wore with white sandals, the wisps of hair that had come down from its knot, the way her hands were clenched and a nerve that was flickering in her jaw. Then he said and put out a hand to cover hers, 'Now will you listen to me, Olivia Lockhart?'

'I...don't know what to say, Ben.'

He smiled slightly. 'Don't say anything, then, until I've explained.'

'But—'

He lifted his hand and touched her lips. 'No, it's my turn.'

'I...'

'Let's sit down,' he suggested.

She hesitated then sank down onto the grass with the skirt of her dress belled out around her. He sat beside her and leant against the trunk of the tree.

'Ben, I—'

'Just hear me out. Then you may speak.' He grimaced but went on immediately. 'I fell in love with you, Olivia. It started as an admiration then became a fascination that took possession of me in a way I hadn't believed could happen. It caused a hunger and a desire to be totally intimate with you in every way and caused me to lose all my cynicism on the subject of what the pressures of marriage could do to what I felt for you—because I know damn well that not being able to have you to live the rest of my life with would be intolerable.'

She stared at him with her lips parted and her grey eyes huge.

He grimaced again. 'What did you think I'd come to say? No, don't answer, as you often say to me. Let me go on.

'Naturally, to discover that this had happened to me when I was engaged to another woman came as something of a shock. And to realize that just about everything else about me was anathema to you, to put it mildly, came as even more of a shock.' He raised a rueful eyebrow.

'It also brought out the worst in me,' he went on. 'But when you steadfastly held to your principles I got over all the knocks to my ego and decided there had to be a way I could prove to you that, despite all the dreadful suspicions you were quite entitled to have about me, I love you, Olivia.'

Their gazes caught and held. 'I didn't plan it, I confess,' he said softly. 'I thought I had my life planned out pretty well. I thought I could work at a marriage with Caiti and the fact that she was fairly dedicated to her acting career would give us—space. And that, as I told you, it might be as good as it could get. The mere *thought* of space between you and I, on the other hand, fills me with dread. These last weeks have been a living hell, for example.'

Olivia swallowed and pushed her fringe aside.

'Could you ever accept,' he said very quietly, 'that I'm not a womanizer, just a poor fool of a man who had no idea what it was really all about until I knocked myself out in your paddock, and met you? Neither am I the kind of monster you took me for business-wise because I couldn't bear to think of you walking away from Wattle Creek, Olivia, and if you really want to we could give our children a hyphenated surname.'

She blinked and her lips curved. 'That is generous—are you asking me to marry you, Ben?'

'I am, but you were going to say something earlier?'

'Yes.' She took a breath and trembled. 'I was going to say that despite your offer I couldn't stay here because it would kill me to have to be in contact with you only on a business partnership basis. You see, losing Wattle in the end became nothing compared to…thinking that I was just a "win some, lose some" proposition for you.'

'That was what little ego I had left talking, Olivia. Plus a belated intimation that I was rushing my fences. My dear—are you sure? I have to tell you I can be diabolical at times—'

'Do you think I don't know that, Ben Bradshaw? It's just, well, I've never sung a man to sleep before—perhaps that's it,' she said helplessly, then they were laughing and in each other's arms kissing hungrily.

'Can I—can I take you somewhere?' he said.

'Right now?'

'Yes, right now.' He stood up and held his hand down to her then led her through the gate to the utility.

'I think I can guess,' she said breathlessly as he drove like the wind and they rattled and bumped over the country. 'Uncle Garth might wonder what we're doing, though.'

He brought the utility to a stop beneath the huge old ghost gums that lined Wattle Creek and looked at her with all the wicked, glinting devilry that he was capable of. 'He won't as it happens.'

Olivia got out. So did he and immediately came round to take her in his arms. 'What do you mean?' she asked.

'He knows full well that—something's on the cards, probably not this precisely but—'

'You told him!'

'I told him that I'd really like the opportunity to mend my fences with you, Olivia,' he said gravely. 'I also brought my mother along; she's dying to meet you—he's giving her a limited tour of the place in the air-conditioned comfort of the Land Rover even as we speak.'

'You are diabolical,' she breathed. 'Were you so sure I—'

'No, my darling.' His eyes changed and they were deadly serious. 'But I wasn't going to let you go without bringing up all the heavy artillery I could.'

'Ben,' she whispered shakenly, 'do I really mean— I mean…?'

But he held her so hard she could barely breathe.

'You asked me where home was, once,' he said later, when they were lying on an old rug from the utility that he'd spread on the grass beside the creek. 'It's here, within you—' he laid his hand on the region of her heart '—and, because you and Wattle are inseparable, it will be home too.'

'That's lovely,' she said softly, 'but I won't hold you to it.'

'What do *you* mean?' He pushed himself up on one elbow and looked down at her frowningly.

'That I'll never again allow a place and bricks and mortar to mean more to me than anything else, that's all. Or, to put it in your terms, my home will be where *your* heart is.'

For a moment he looked comically put out. 'So much for grand gestures,' he said slowly, then laughed. 'Do you think I was trying to play Lord Bountiful?'

'Not at all,' she replied innocently.

'Well, I was but once again you've brought me back to earth.' He looked at her ruefully.

She sat up with a secret little smile. 'Can I tell you something?'

'Of course.'

'One morning, a few weeks ago and only a day after our first—encounter, right here...' She stopped and looked around at the dappled shade. The creek wasn't as full as it had been that day but was still running and the birds were singing and there were crickets and cicadas chorusing shrilly. Beyond the shade the landscape was shimmering in a haze of heat.

'I remember it well,' he said gravely, and sat up so that their shoulders were touching.

She glanced at him with a tinge of colour in her cheeks at what she saw in his eyes but went on steadily, 'I woke up that morning—in love.' She paused as she heard his swiftly indrawn breath. 'I told myself I shouldn't be, I barely knew you, but I did know you could be lethally charming and I very much suspected that most women would find you hard to resist. It didn't make any difference.'

'Olivia—'

She put her hand over his. 'It's my turn, Ben. Nothing I told myself altered the fact that the world had become a different place for me, a better place. My heart was light, I was filled with a sense of anticipation, I felt like a girl in love for the very first time. I went out as the sun was rising and picked myself some flowers and knew that nothing I did could change how I felt about you.'

He sighed and put his arm around her. 'Then you got one shock on top of another.'

She laid her head on his shoulder. 'I felt beat, bushed and battered, yes,' she confessed. 'And angry, deeply angry, but it didn't change. Even when I told you I couldn't see any future for us, I was still in love with you. Far too much to be able to accept anything less from you.'

'My darling Olivia,' he said bleakly, 'I—

'I'm telling you this, Ben, not to make you feel bad,' she said with a faint smile, 'but just to let you know that you *are* my Lord Bountiful, you make the very air I breathe so rarefied, it makes me giddy just to be close to you—so don't feel downcast because your grand gesture fell a little flat.'

He was speechless for a moment then they were laughing together, he exultantly, until he said, 'There's only one problem with that—I ought to take you back to lunch all proper and correct but I don't think I'm capable of it now.'

'I'd be most disappointed if you didn't kiss me first,' she murmured.

'Ah, there was a bit more to it that I had in mind.'

'Perhaps we should take our clothes off first this time?' she suggested, entirely seriously, apart from the little glint in her eye.

'Good thinking,' he replied. 'By the way I checked that Bonnie was in her stall—should she suddenly recall her chaperon duties.'

Olivia glanced around and said ruefully, 'I wish you hadn't reminded me of that. There is a pair of little people who have the unfortunate habit of turning up—anywhere.'

'You can't be referring to Sonia and Ryan!' He looked shocked.

'Strangely enough I am.'

'Then you must be a mind-reader. Steve is giving all the kids a flight over the property as it happens.'

Olivia turned to him, her eyes alight with love and laughter. 'You are diabolical, Ben Bradshaw! I doubt you had any intention of taking me back to lunch all proper and correct.'

'Well, possibly not, but you know what an impatient type of guy I am.'

'So—there's nothing for it but to humour you?' She eyed him then stood up and issued a challenge. 'Bet I can beat you in!'

'I knew, I knew you'd be like this,' he said unsteadily.

They'd frolicked in the water, splashing each other, then come together with all laughter banished as desire gripped them.

'Like what?' she asked breathlessly.

'Pale, satiny.' He held her away from him and his gaze travelled down her glistening body from her small, firm breasts, the slight swell of her belly to the triangle of darker curls at the base of it, then the sweep of her legs. 'Purely feminine under your tough jillaroo exterior—and I mean that only in a mental sense.'

'I have to tell you, Ben, that I feel exquisitely feminine when you look at me like that but also, I always knew you were something of an Adonis under your clothes.'

'You had the advantage of me, Olivia. You always did.'

'I don't know about that.' She smoothed her hands over his shoulders then down his chest and he cupped her bottom. 'But I can also remember doing something like this.' She raised her arms above her head. 'Because the way I felt when you ran your hands down me was—something else, and I had my clothes on then.'

He did it again and said, 'I may not have to tell you what it does to me.'

'Oh, Ben,' she gasped as he folded her into his arms then picked her up and carried her out of the creek to lay her on the blanket.

It was something she said several more times as he claimed her, with various shades of meaning in her voice, desire, rapture, pleading when the pleasure was almost more than she could bear and, finally, pure ecstasy.

They were quiet for a time afterwards, supremely

shaken in Olivia's case by the intensity of their love-making.

'All right?' he said at last.

'No,' she whispered.

He looked at her with concern.

She touched her fingertips to the scar on his temple. 'I'm actually better than I've ever felt in my life,' she murmured, 'just a bit stunned.'

He buried his head between her breasts for a long moment then kissed her lips. 'The feeling is mutual.'

'How are we going to…meet and greet people?'

'With extreme difficulty if you mean what I think you mean. How will we be able to tear our thoughts from us and this?' He drew his hand down her back and let it lie on her hip.

She cleared her throat and moved her body against his. 'Yes.'

'We could leave them a note,' he suggested.

She smiled but it died and it shook her even more to see an answering smile in his eyes that died just as swiftly as hers had. But he said gently after a long moment, 'How would it be if we broke the news, made some arrangements and pleaded for their indulgence? Some immediate time on our own in other words.'

'I think that would be…about as much as I could handle,' she said softly. 'I didn't know, you see…' She stopped and looked at him a little helplessly.

'Well, that's where I had the advantage of you, my Livvie Lockhart. I did know it would be like this—it couldn't have been any other way between us. And what's more, don't imagine it will ever be any different.'

Her eyes danced for a moment. 'For a non-believer you've become the opposite, Benedict Arnold.'

'I wondered if you'd ever call me that again.'

'I...well, I wondered when you signed that very impersonal note you left me at Mermaid Beach whether it might be a secret sign but then I told myself it was only wishful thinking.'

'There were times when I told myself it was wishful thinking that you'd even notice how I'd signed myself.'

Olivia breathed softly, 'I not only noticed, I kissed it—before I tore it up.'

He grimaced. 'That sounds a lot like you, Olivia.' And once again they were laughing together and gradually she felt more normal and as if she might just be able to face the world.

She told him this but added gravely, 'I could need a bit of help if I'm to be anything approaching proper and correct.'

'Anything I can do at all?' he replied promptly.

'Let me go for one thing—I don't seem to have the will to free myself.'

'You'll never know how hard this is going to be,' he said with a wicked little grin, and kissed her lingeringly. But then he did release her and, taking her hand, helped her up and led her back into the creek.

'Oh, no!' she groaned. 'This is where it all started!'

'Place your trust in wise old Wattle Creek,' he advised as they started to scoop water over themselves.

Then they found a rough old towel in the back of

the utility and dried themselves off and put their clothes on.

But he took her hand once they were dressed and she was just about to get into the utility. 'You said something about being a non-believer earlier, Olivia.'

'Yes...'

He looked down at her and the world of dappled sunlight, bird song and the chuckle of the creek receded. 'I believe in you more than anything I've believed in in my life.'

'Ben, I love you,' she replied. 'We're home where we belong.'

He raised her hand and kissed her knuckles then they looked at each other with their lips twitching. 'No,' he said.

'No,' she agreed. 'We should be strong. Think of my poor uncle and your poor mother waiting up at the house in possibly dreadful suspense.'

'I am...trying to. You know,' he said thoughtfully, 'it will give me great pleasure, incidentally, to prove my poor mother, who is not poor at all but extremely opinionated and interfering, wrong. She was so convinced I was jaded, cynical, capricious and all the rest of it.'

'Come to think of it,' Olivia said, 'it will delight me to prove to my uncle that I'm not on the shelf and a born spinster who can only paint flowers and care about a cattle station!'

'Should we hop to it, then?'

'Let's,' Olivia agreed joyfully.

*An electric chemistry with a disturbingly
familiar stranger…
A reawakening of passions long forgotten…
And a compulsive desire to get to know
this stranger all over again!*

Because

**What the memory has lost,
the body never forgets**

In Harlequin Presents®
over the coming months look out for:

BACK IN THE MARRIAGE BED
by Penny Jordan
On sale September, #2129

SECRET SEDUCTION
by Susan Napier
On sale October, #2135

THE SICILIAN'S MISTRESS
by Lynne Graham
On sale November, #2139

Available wherever Harlequin books are sold.

Visit us at www.eHarlequin.com

HPAMN

If you enjoyed what you just read,
then we've got an offer you can't resist!

Take 2 bestselling love stories FREE!
Plus get a FREE surprise gift!

Clip this page and mail it to Harlequin Reader Service®

IN U.S.A.
3010 Walden Ave.
P.O. Box 1867
Buffalo, N.Y. 14240-1867

IN CANADA
P.O. Box 609
Fort Erie, Ontario
L2A 5X3

YES! Please send me 2 free Harlequin Presents® novels and my free surprise gift. Then send me 6 brand-new novels every month, which I will receive months before they're available in stores. In the U.S.A., bill me at the bargain price of $3.34 plus 25¢ delivery per book and applicable sales tax, if any*. In Canada, bill me at the bargain price of $3.74 plus 25¢ delivery per book and applicable taxes**. That's the complete price and a savings of at least 10% off the cover prices—what a great deal! I understand that accepting the 2 free books and gift places me under no obligation ever to buy any books. I can always return a shipment and cancel at any time. Even if I never buy another book from Harlequin, the 2 free books and gift are mine to keep forever. So why not take us up on our invitation. You'll be glad you did!

106 HEN C22Q
306 HEN C22R

Name _____ (PLEASE PRINT)

Address _____ Apt.#

City _____ State/Prov. _____ Zip/Postal Code

* Terms and prices subject to change without notice. Sales tax applicable in N.Y.
** Canadian residents will be charged applicable provincial taxes and GST.
  All orders subject to approval. Offer limited to one per household.
  ® are registered trademarks of Harlequin Enterprises Limited.

PRES00   ©1998 Harlequin Enterprises Limited

HARLEQUIN

Duets™

Pick up a Harlequin Duets™
from August–October 2000
and receive $1.00 off the
original cover price. *

Experience the "lighter side of love"
in a Harlequin Duets™.
This unbeatable value just became
irresistible with our special introductory
price of $4.99 U.S./$5.99 CAN. for
2 Brand-New, Full-Length
Romantic Comedies.

Offer available for a limited time only.
Offer applicable only to Harlequin Duets™.
*Original cover price is $5.99 U.S./$6.99 CAN.

Visit us at www.eHarlequin.com   HDMKD

Your Romantic Books—find them at

www.eHarlequin.com

Visit the *Author's Alcove*

> Find the most complete information anywhere on your favorite author.

> Try your hand in the Writing Round Robin— contribute a chapter to an online book in the making.

Enter the *Reading Room*

> Experience an interactive novel—help determine the fate of a story being created now by one of your favorite authors.

> Join one of our reading groups and discuss your favorite book.

Drop into *Shop eHarlequin*

> Find the latest releases—read an excerpt or write a review for this month's Harlequin top sellers.

> Try out our amazing search feature—tell us your favorite theme, setting or time period and we'll find a book that's perfect for you.

All this and more available at

www.eHarlequin.com
on Women.com Networks

HEYRB1

*Don't miss
an exciting opportunity
to save on the purchase of
Harlequin and Silhouette books!*

Buy any two Harlequin or
Silhouette books and save
$10.00 off future Harlequin
and Silhouette purchases

OR

buy any three
Harlequin or Silhouette books
and save **$20.00 off** future
Harlequin and Silhouette purchases.

*Watch for details
coming in October 2000!*

PHQ400

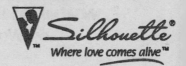